The Sheik's Rescue

The Del Taran

Elizabeth Lennox

Table of Contents

Chapter 1

Smothering a curse, Calista turned her head away, not wanting to watch as the tall, handsome man stepped up onto the stage. The applause was almost deafening, the crowd cheering for the man. But Calista didn't get it. She didn't understand why these people loved him so much. Point of fact, she hated him.

Unfortunately, she was also engaged to him.

Oh, he was handsome enough, she thought, turning back to look at him as he greeted the speaker, shaking the other man's hand and commenting on whatever the speaker was saying to him. Goran was the epitome of "tall, dark and handsome". Add in charisma that was off the charts and, intellectually, Calista could understand why everyone loved him.

Everyone else, she corrected!

She watched with her professional, polite mask firmly in place when the crowds continued to cheer, even standing up as if the man had done something extraordinary.

Calista sighed, trying hard not to rub her temples as a headache started to make itself known. She was just tired, she told herself. As soon as she left here, she could head to the airport and go home. Or maybe she should take a moment to tell her fiancé that she wasn't going to marry him before she boarded the flight home. Yes, that was probably a wise thing to do. Better to end this annoying engagement before she left. That way, she could go back home and leave all this tension behind.

Why in the world had she agreed to such a farcical engagement in the first place?

Oh yeah. He'd kissed her. After her brother's wedding, the man had asked her to dance. And that dance had led to a quiet, tingling stroll

1

through a moonlit garden and...then he'd kissed her. A week later, through phone calls that had almost felt like a diplomatic negotiation, she'd agreed to his proposal.

A proposal over the phone should have been her first clue, Calista thought.

But she'd kept remembering that kiss in the moonlight!

That kiss had been...wow! She'd kissed men during her college years. But when Sheik Goran el Istara, proud and powerful leader of Skyla, had kissed her, she'd seen sparks flying through the air, even though her eyes had been closed. It was almost as if she'd come alive for the first time in her life with that kiss, her whole body tingling and ener-vated, wanting...wanting something she'd never even known existed!

Even now, she could remember the singe of her lips, the sparks in her fingers and toes as he'd kissed her that day so long ago. She'd remem-bered thinking, "Yes! Finally! This was the man!"

Unfortunately, there hadn't been any additional kisses since that magi-cal night. Every interaction since then had felt...clinical. Passionless! Even worse, every conversation with Goran had felt like an interview, as if he were somehow testing her intelligence and ensuring that her opinions aligned with his own. Those conversations had been difficult as she'd tried very hard to remain diplomatic while still being true to her personal beliefs. All of those conversational struggles had angered her because...well, she'd felt as if she'd failed somehow. She could see the disappointment in his eyes. She'd felt his frustration, even if he didn't touch her again.

Sighing, Calista focused on the man now standing at the podium. The excited crowd resumed their seats and Calista sank gratefully into the chair on the stage. A hush fell over the crowd as everyone waited to hear what the great Sheik Goran was going to say next!

Knowing that the press was in the back of the room, their cameras clicking away and video recording every expression, every movement of her body which would eventually be analyzed later, Calista pasted a polite smile to her face, shifted her knees towards Goran and demurely crossed her legs at the ankles. Feigning interest, she lifted her chin, try-ing very hard to listen to the words. Unfortunately, the speakers were facing towards the audience. Calista only heard every third or fourth word so she wasn't sure what the man was saying!

When she'd first met Goran el Istra, Calista had thought that the man was dashing and daring and...and he'd taken her breath away! They'd talked several times and then...goodness, that kiss! One kiss and she'd melted against him! When he'd asked her to marry him, she'd under-stood that they didn't really know each other. He was a powerful ruler

2

and she was the sister to another powerful leader. Goran didn't have time to court a woman, to have endless conversations and take her out to dinner. He didn't have the time for all of the dates and rituals that would give them time to get to know one another. But after that kiss, Calista had believed that they could work out any issues. She'd believed! So she'd entered into the engagement thinking that her life would be filled with interesting adventures.

The reality was that her life was now filled with formal dinners and boring conversations with tedious diplomats and dreary world leaders, pompous business executives and mind-numbing social events. It was filled with rules and decorous protocols and monotonous efforts to...to get away from the man! Good grief, Calista had become an expert at coming up with reasons to avoid the man!

Unfortunately, tonight had been one of those events she couldn't escape. Tonight, Goran's assistant had called Calista's assistant, asking if their schedules would allow a joint public appearance. Hence, her presence here on the stage, wearing a sedate...uh, boring...ivory suit and boring ivory heels, her hair pulled back into a sedate chignon de-signed not to offend anyone. There would be no hand holding, no brief touches and absolutely no kissing during this trip to Skyla. Everything was strictly...yawn...business.

Calista didn't want this. She didn't want to be the public wife of a man who didn't want to touch her. She didn't want to be the woman who walked by his side, never truly loving her husband.

She'd seen how her older brother, Astir, loved his wife Rachel. Those two were sweetly, madly in love. They couldn't seem to stop touching each other and Calista couldn't count the number of times she'd caught those two in some alcove making out or asked if her oldest brother was available, only to find that his office door was locked, with Rachel in-side. It didn't take a rocket scientist to figure out what they were doing in Astir's office!

Damn Astir! Damn him for showing her what she would be miss-ing if she married a dud like Goran! She didn't want to be constantly smothering a yawn during her marriage. She wanted...passion! She wanted excitement! She wanted to be challenged by her husband and to challenge him back! She wanted...someone other than the powerful world leader who seemed more interested in his next economic policy than in her!

Would Goran even notice if she just...puff...disappeared? Would he even care? Probably not, she thought as Goran shifted on his feet, his speech continuing. For a moment, she wondered what he would say. What was this conference even about? Calista had no idea. Her assistant had put this event on her schedule without asking, then had apologized profusely when Calista had grumbled about the obligation. Granted, it had been over a year since she'd agreed to the engagement, so it was time for them to set a date for the wedding. But every time someone mentioned setting a date, Calista felt as if she were being sentenced to a prison term!

Hence, why Calista was going to tell Goran that she couldn't marry him. Today! Before she got on that plane to fly home, she would be a single woman again! No way would she subject herself to a lifetime of his boring conversations about economic policies or military spending or...or whatever yawn-worthy topic he brought up during their next meal together.

And yeah, a formal dinner was on the agenda tonight. Alone. With him!

Little did he know that she was going to dump him! She'd be very kind and tell him it was "all about her" and that she couldn't see tying him down with her, with someone who had "issues". She wasn't sure what those issues were, other than the need to not be bored out of her mind for the next fifty years. But she'd come up with something. Something horrible. Maybe a disease? Yes! Yes, a wasting disease that couldn't be cured. Of course, in a few months, or maybe a year, she could announce that she'd been cured. No, she'd have to wait until after Goran's wedding to someone else before she was cured.

Tuning out his words, she couldn't bear to listen to yet another speech about building another university or bridge or hospital or...whatever. Those were all very necessary, wonderful accomplishments. But did she really need to be here? Or even better than her absence, wouldn't it be amazing to be part of the planning and implementation stages of those accomplishments?

Goran finished his speech and turned, looking at the woman sitting primly on the stage behind him. How the hell had he been so wrong about her? Calista was...uptight. After that one kiss they'd shared so many months ago, he'd had high hopes for their marriage. But she carried that "don't touch me" attitude around with her, no matter where they were. They could be completely alone or in a crowd of people and Calista's body language screamed "Don't touch me!"

She was a stunningly beautiful woman with dark, silky hair that he knew would cascade over her delicate shoulders...if she ever lightened up enough to release it from the tight knot she put it into every time he saw her. He also knew that she had a lust-worthy figure. He'd felt her curves, experienced that body shivering against him during that one kiss.

But every time he saw her now, she was wearing stiff, formal jackets that masked her curves, hiding every delectable inch of her from his view. All he could see were the lovely cat eyes and soft, full lips that he imagined kissing...except that every time he looked at her, she seemed to be pulling from him, those full, kissable lips in a frown that warned him off. Even today, he was definitely getting the "hands off" vibe from the lovely Princess Calista.

Walking over to her, Goran wondered what she would do if he reached out and messed up her perfectly coifed hair. Or if he kissed her? Would she shudder with revulsion? Was it just him that she didn't like? Or was it all of humanity? He'd wondered briefly if she might prefer women, because every time he almost touched her, Calista backed out of the way, silently announcing that she wanted nothing to do with him.

Tonight though...tonight he was going to tell her that their engagement needed to end. He was going to tell her that...that it wasn't her, that he needed to focus on the business of running his country and he didn't want to put her into a situation in which she felt less than... whatever. He didn't care if she believed him or not, he wasn't marrying a woman who didn't want him. There was no way in hell he wanted to live the life of a monk!

Calista was a startlingly beautiful woman, he'd grant her that much. Her soft, creamy skin and her long, dark hair...hair that was always contained with pins and hairspray so that nothing, not even a hurricane, could mess up her style. And her clothes? Her outfits were the epitome of an ice queen! That ivory suit she'd chosen to wear today... what the hell? The color suited her creamy skin, but it also made her look...frozen. It didn't help that her facial expressions barely moved!

No. Just...no way in hell was he marrying this woman! Their one kiss had fooled him into thinking that Calista was a passionate woman. But after that, she'd silently warned him that there was nothing passionate, or even warm, about her. Every conversational gambit he'd offered had been shut down with polite, politically correct answers and a politely cold smile. He had no idea who the real woman was underneath all of that ice.

She was cold and emotionless, with none of the spirit or spunk that he'd been hoping was beneath that startlingly beautiful exterior. She couldn't even converse about...anything other than politics! Oh, she was well versed in many of the political issues both of their countries were striving to handle right now. But there was more to life than politics! What did she think and feel and dream about? What was the real Calista like? And why the hell did she constantly bring up those tedious conversational topics when there was so much more that they needed to discuss?!

Tonight, he told himself. Tonight, he'd break off their engagement. He'd let her tell the press anything she wanted, just as long as he didn't have to live with her for the rest of his life!

Sitting down in the chair next to her, he gritted his teeth when Calista shifted her legs to the right, as far away from any part of him as possible.

Just to irritate her, Goran stretched his arm out along the back of her chair, keeping a blank expression on his features when her body tensed.

He didn't care. This would be their last public appearance together. Of course, he'd have to talk with Astir about the issue. Sheik Astir wasn't just Calista's brother. He was also Goran's friend. As leaders of neighboring countries, they'd had disagreements over the years, but they'd always remained friends and had been able to work out their differences.

Goran hoped that this wouldn't be the issue that dissolved their friendship. Goran had been the best man at Astir's wedding. He would talk to his friend and explain the situation. Goran wanted a marriage just like Astir's and he wouldn't settle for anything less.

He definitely wouldn't settle for the cold, emotionless relationship that, apparently, Calista had been anticipating.

"Your plan had better work!" Harvey Neville snarled. "I don't want a catastrophe like the last idiot created. No collapsed buildings, no missing investigators and get the damn mineral deposit out of the earth and to my factories!"

Neville watched as the former gangster sitting in his office barely controlled his sneer after that tirade. "My plan will work." Ned Afrehoster asserted firmly. He sat in the chair, cool and calm after explaining how he would distract the Skyla government so Neville's mining equipment could move into position. They'd attack the efiasia deposit from a different angle this time since the Silarian government was still trying to investigate the village that had caved into the earth during the last mining attempt.

Neville leaned back in his massive leather chair, lacing his gnarled fingers together. "What if it doesn't?"

Ned lifted a dark eyebrow. "If you don't trust me, then just say so now and I'll get out of the way so you can hire someone you do trust."

Neville snorted. "I don't trust anyone but myself!" He sighed, a rattling sound coming from his lungs like a death rattle, and shifted slightly to ease the ache in his old bones. "When will it happen?"

Ned shrugged, his mouth shifting casually. "Soon."

That one word response obviously irritated Neville, which only delighted Ned. "I want details!" Neville roared. "I need that mineral deposit and I need it fast! If you want me to trust you, then you're damn well going to give me details!"

Ned chuckled. "You already told me that you only trust yourself. So nothing I say is going to engender trust." He stood up, jerking the sides of his suit jacket as he looked down at the older man. "It will happen soon. But let me assure you," he started off, leaning forward on the old man's desk, "if I fail, then you'd better not come after me the way you did Kipsinger." The warning was given in a soft, threatening voice. "He was already in prison. Having him stabbed in the back was cowardly."

Neville's face contorted with rage. "He failed me!"

Ned pushed away, straightening once again. "Whatever. I won't fail."

With that assurance given, Ned turned and walked out of the man's office.

Chapter 2

Calista shifted to the right, out of the way as the eager crowd surged forward. The interminable conference had finally ended. All she wanted to do now was to head back to her hotel suite and soak in a hot bath! Her back hurt, her legs hurt and even her ankles hurt since she'd had to remain on that stage with her legs crossed demurely at the ankles. She wondered if the rest of the world had any idea how hard it was to keep one's legs crossed at the ankles like that, never shifting, never changing positions for fear that some enterprising and overly observant photographer, or just some jerk with a cell phone, might capture the instant when her shifting legs revealed something that the rest of the world didn't need to see.

Men didn't need to worry about that! Goran had worn slacks to this conference! He'd shifted back and forth in his chair, crossing and uncrossing his legs whichever way he needed to shift in order to be comfortable! The jerk! And now, she couldn't even get away to relax. She had to stand here, smiling like an idiot while the press yelled out questions to him. Why couldn't she head out to the vehicle? Why did she have to stand here? It wasn't as if she had some sort of interest in this conference! In truth, she hadn't heard anything that anyone had said during any of the speeches. She'd been too absorbed in plotting out what she'd do once she'd told Goran that she wanted to end the engagement. She was also eager to see the furious look in his eyes when she told him the news. Just one little spark of...any emotion!

Of course, he probably wouldn't be furious. The man didn't have any emotions underneath that handsome façade, she suspected. Oh, he was intelligent enough. Probably too intelligent! The man didn't have a heart. He had a calculator where his heart was supposed to be! One that continuously calculated the profits or cost of one thing or another.

The man could spout facts and figures unlike anyone she'd ever known! Some might even call the man brilliant.

She called him a bore!

Except for that one, damn kiss!

Smothering yet another sigh, she shifted her clutch purse from her hands so that it was now tucked under one arm. She tried to take the weight off of one foot, but the pressure on the second foot was too much. She really shouldn't have worn these heels today. She should have worn the other pair that was more broken in. Now she'd have a blister because these shoes were too tight at the toes. Darn it, when was the man going to shut up?! Couldn't he delegate the talking points to one of his subordinates? Why did Sheik Goran have to answer all of the reporters' questions?!

Maybe he'd shut up if she flipped one of her shoes towards his head.

Calista banished the thought, because all of her shoes were specially made. Unfortunately, her mental efforts worked for about five seconds. But then Sheik Goran, her "beloved" fiancé, took yet another question from the group of reporters and the image popped back into her mind. What would he do if she just...flipped her foot up? Maybe that was something she'd have to practice at home for future use. She could draw a target on one of the walls in her suite and practice flipping the shoe from her foot to the circle. Of course, she'd have to be careful about which shoes she flipped. She had several "special" shoes, including the pair she was currently wearing. It wouldn't do to have her special shoes going astray of her target!

The man in question turned and...stared at her. Calista stared back, not sure why he had that startled look on his features but...for some silly reason, the look caused her heart rate to accelerate. She didn't want that. Calista really didn't want to feel...anything...for Sheik Goran. All she wanted was to leave this crowded place, have a brief but polite dinner with the man where she gave him the news of their breakup, then drive to the airport where a plane was on standby for her. She'd climb on board, wave to whatever intrepid reporters followed her all the way to the airport, then step into the cool interior of the plane. She knew that her favorite flight attendant, John, would have a chilled glass of white wine ready for her. He'd hand it to her seconds before the pilot started down the runway for takeoff. God bless Johnny! He always knew what she needed!

Unlike some men!

Feeling strange, almost nervous, Calista's chin went up a notch. Unknowingly, one dark eyebrow lifted as well.

"Your Highness?"

Calista turned, trying to dismiss Goran's odd reaction, but focused on the nervous woman standing in front of her.

"Yes?" she asked, relieved to have something to do other than stand here alone feeling awkward.

"I'm sorry to disturb you," she said in a low voice, then she paused to glance nervously at the body guards that were glaring at her. "I just..." she sighed, clenching her hand tightly together. "I was just wondering if you could mention to..." she tilted her head slightly, indicating Goran. "We're...I..." she stumbled, sighing in frustration.

"Go ahead," Calista urged, gently touching the woman's arm.

The woman smiled briefly. "Thank you. You're very kind." She seemed to pause long enough to pull herself together. "It's just that... well, strange things are happening near my town. There are lots of strange noises at night and bit trucks. After what happened in Silar, with the town collapsing and all, I was wondering if...maybe someone could look into the issue?"

Calista tried to hide her surprise with an encouraging smile and nodded. "Of course. Strange nighttime noises doesn't sound very savory." Her smile widened towards the woman. "I'll whisper in a few people's ears."

The woman's relief was apparent on her features and she gushed out, "Oh, thank you Your Highness!" And then she was gone! The woman simply spun around on her heel and hurried out through a side door.

Calista watched, confused because...well, what town? Did the woman live here in Skyla or in Silar? Was the woman asking for Calista to mention the issue to Astir or Goran? And...how many trucks? What kinds of sounds? She glanced at her guards, both of whom shrugged, obviously equally confused.

Calista almost asked one of the guards to go after the woman and get more information, but Goran's conversation had ended and he was shaking the other man's hand.

He walked over to her, his towering height causing him to look down at her even though she was wearing four-inch heels. Never mind that those heels might have been tossed against the back of his head. Or that they were now hurting her feet. These heels gave her the much needed height so she didn't feel so painfully short while standing next to him.

"Are you ready to leave?" he asked, his tone one of sardonic...amusement? What the hell did he have to be amused about?

Calista dismissed the strange woman, wondering if she'd just been punked. "Only if you've finished all of your business," she replied, her voice saccharine sweet. Calista added an overly bright smile, batting her eye lashes for effect.

"I'm ready," he said. Without another word, he shifted so that she could precede him out the door to the waiting limousines. Calista ducked into the back of the limousine and scooted over, leaving at least two feet of space so that there was no risk that he might inadvertently touch her.

Goran gritted his teeth, wishing that he could figure Calista out. When he'd turned around a moment ago to find her smiling, a soft, gentle look to her eyes and a softness around her mouth, he'd been... enchanted once again.

Unfortunately, the lovely expression was fleeting. The blank look quickly descended back into place, but this time, she added in that sarcastic lift of her eyebrow.

He watched as Calista ducked into the back of the limousine and he couldn't stop his eyes from looking at her derriere. He might not like her personality, but Goran had no issues with her ass! Princess Calista had a damn fine ass! One that he'd like to spank. Hard! He'd love to teach her a lesson, to show her that he wasn't going to endure those blank facial expressions.

Sighing, he paused before he followed her into the limousine. Goran wanted to growl when he noticed her sitting so far away, but instead, his phone rang and he answered the call.

For the next fifteen minutes, he dealt with the numerous issues that his assistant needed to go over with him. He really was going to have to find a new assistant because Samir seemed to struggle to make any kind of decision on his own. Plus, too many of the problems weren't getting filtered. Ninety percent of the questions Samir had for Goran should have been diverted to someone else on the staff and Samir should know these issues already.

When Goran finally ended the call, he turned to face Calista, determined to start the conversation, gently, that would end their relationship.

"I apologize for the phone call," he said to her, tucking the phone into his pocket, but he turned it off so that he could focus on her.

"It seems that you have many issues to handle," she commented. Goran got the impression that she wasn't very interested.

"Yes, but I shouldn't need to handle most of them. I'm going to have to find a new assistant. Samir has been with me for six months. I thought he had more potential, but apparently, he hasn't picked up the various nuances of his job yet."

Goran clenched his teeth when the lovely, cold-hearted woman simply turned her head and said, "That's a shame. Hopefully, you can find a different position for him in..."

She wasn't able to finish that sentence because a loud explosion erupted, ending not just the conversation, but also his consciousness. A searing pain traveled up the back of his neck and then...nothing!

Chapter 3

"Wake up!"

Goran groaned and tried to lift his head but a searing pain stopped his efforts. He felt heavy and...someone kept kicking him.

"Wake up, you monster-sized human!"

He would have laughed at that ridiculous insult if his head wasn't throbbing so painfully. His mouth felt dry and his arms...why couldn't he move his arms? What the hell was going on? And what was that god-awful smell?!

"Ugh!" The voice sounded like Calista's, but Goran couldn't imagine her being so angry. Anger implied emotions and passions! Princess Calista was one of the most lifeless women he'd ever had the misery of knowing. Although, "knowing" wasn't possible. Calista was too diplomatically polite and too introverted for anyone to really "know" her. So who the hell was muttering a series of expletives that would make a sailor blush?

Another kick, this time to his hips, startled him enough so that he lifted his head. Unfortunately, his eyes felt as if they were glued shut. He forced his eyelids to open, just a crack, because the bright light burned the retinas. Quickly, he closed his eyes again, using his other senses to try and figure out what was going on.

Ties. His hands were tied behind his back. That would explain why he couldn't move his arms. It would also explain the burning sensation in his shoulders.

"Darn it, Goran! You'd think that someone of your size would have a bit more resiliency!"

Was she still complaining about his size? He wanted to laugh, since Calista...and yeah, he knew that it was his lovely, cold fiancée now that he recognized her voice as well as the sweet scent of her perfume...was

13

berating him for his size? He hadn't realized that his size was something that she'd hated about him. He'd thought she'd liked his height! Contrary woman!

"Will you please shake it off and wake up?"

That's when he heard the panic in her voice. Reacting to that, he once again lifted his head, forcing his eyelids to open so that he could see her and give her some small measure of reassurance. They'd be fine, he wanted to tell her, but his mouth was too dry. And he couldn't figure out what the hell was going on.

"Where are we?"

Calista's head swiveled around, her big, brown eyes panicked and she shifted her adorable ass along the rough wood of...where the hell were they?

"Pretend you're not awake!" she hissed, shifting her body again. "Do it now!"

Reacting not just to the panic, but also the heavy footsteps outside of the doorway, he let his head bob downwards again. It wasn't hard to fake being "out" since his whole body ached and his head felt as if it might explode from the pain jabbing at every corner of his brain.

A fraction of a second after he let his head flop back down, the heavy, wooden door opened up.

"Who are you talking to?" a male voice demanded.

"Him!" she snapped to whoever was standing in the doorway.

More shuffling footsteps and Goran concentrated on appearing unconscious. "He is awake?"

A long sigh followed that question. "I wish. But whatever was in that syringe was too much for him. He still hasn't moved even when I kick him."

The male voice laughed, but a second later, the door slammed shut. Goran waited for Calista to give him the signal that he could lift his head again. But slowly, as he waited for her signal, he realized several things. First, his hands were tied with one of those plastic zip ties. His feet were bound as well and they'd taken his shoes. Also, one of his ribs might be broken. But other than that, he was fine. Well, besides the splitting headache! Which was a pretty significant issue.

Goran waited another several beats, then lifted his head and forced his eyes to open once again. "What the hell is going on?" he whispered, not wanting the guards to come back and find him awake.

Calista rolled her eyes and he once again had the insane desire to pull her over his lap and spank her sexy ass! How dare she roll her eyes at him!

He would have done it, too. If his damn hands weren't bound behind his back!

"Take my shoe," she whispered, thrusting an ivory shod foot towards him. The stiletto heel was quite nice, but...!

"I'm not in the mood to play footsie at the moment, Calista," he growled, wishing he could shove her pretty foot off of his lap. Again, the bound hands were really pissing him off!

"Don't be an ass!" she hissed at him. "Take the heel and pull!"

"Why the hell would I do that?"

Calista sighed, the sound coming out as if she was reaching for her last reserves of patience. "Look, Goran. I know that there isn't any love lost between us. If we are perfectly honest with each other, we probably hate each other. But right now, we're in a bit of a bind, literally and figuratively. And at this particular moment, I need you to pull the blade out of the heel of my shoe, then hand it to me so that I can cut through these stupid plastic ties." She paused there, staring at him with fury radiating from every fiber of her body. "After we get out of this mess, then we can figure out a way to extricate ourselves from the most tedious engagement two people have ever had to deal with. Okay?"

Goran wanted to argue about the tedious description, but at the moment, he really wanted to get out of the bindings. "Give me the damn shoe," he snapped, then shifted his body so that her foot reached behind him where his hands were bound. It took mere seconds for him to get to the shoe and a moment later, he pulled at the heel to discover that there really was a knife hidden inside. "There are hidden depths to you," he commented, then immediately started to saw away at the plastic ties. "I never knew that."

She rolled her eyes, again, before snapping, "If you weren't such a...!" She stopped abruptly, pressing her lips together as if that was the only thing holding back her angry words.

"What?" he demanded a second after the plastic tie broke under the knife's blade. "I'd love to hear what you think of me." He shifted around, sliced through the plastic tie around his ankles, then rolled to his feet. Walking behind her, he used the blade and, with a brisk snap, her hands were freed as well.

"No, you really don't," she grumbled, then reached out to take the knife back from him.

"I'll hold onto this until we're out of here," he told her, pulling the knife from her reach.

She glared at him and, once again, he had the almost uncontrollable urge to flip her over so he could spank her! Where the hell had the quiet, complacent...boring...woman gone? And who the hell was this angry, spitting tiger?

Granted, the fire in her eyes was actually turning him on, even though this was the worst time to realize that the woman wasn't quite the boring ice princess he'd originally thought. Perhaps there was a fire underneath that beautifully cold exterior.

"Give me my knife!" she snapped. "You probably don't know how to use it. But I do! I've been trained in several forms of fighting. If you'll just stand behind me, then I can get us out of here."

Stand behind her? What the hell was she talking about?

"Calista, if you could..." He stopped when she lifted a hand to halt whatever he'd been about to spew next. "Quiet!"

Heavy footsteps came down the hallway and Goran moved swiftly and quietly in sock-feet around the small space, placing himself behind the door.

It opened swiftly and, after checking through the crack in the doorway and the door frame to make sure there wasn't another guard waiting, Goran shifted on the balls of his feet, turning, grabbing the man's arm and twisting until the guard's arm pulled out of his shoulder socket. Before the man could scream, Goran's fingers pressed against the muscles and nerve endings on his shoulder, creating a dual reaction of absolute silence as well as knocking the man unconscious. He fell heavily to the floor, with Goran guiding him so that he didn't make too much noise.

"Close the door," he ordered softly, then quickly began undressing the man, starting with his boots. Looking at them carefully, Goran acknowledged that they were a bit smaller than he'd prefer, but slightly small boots were better than nothing at all. Goran was fully aware that kidnappers generally took a person's shoes in order to deter them from escaping as well as to slow them down if they tried. In this instance, the kidnappers were stupid to have left Calista with her shoes. But even he had to admit that he wouldn't have thought that a pair of heels would be a threat. Heels that high would definitely slow a woman down. It was very difficult to run in a pair of stilettos. He made a mental note to tell his guards that all women's heels should be examined in the future for potential weapons.

"That was..." When Calista paused, he lifted his head, looking down at her stunned eyes.

"What?" he prompted, enjoying her surprise after her previous command that he simply stay back so she could do the rough stuff.

Calista shook her head and stepped back. "Just...I didn't know that..."

"That I could fight?" he asked, then flipped the knife around, handing it to her so that he could reach down to lace up the boots. "Why don't you take his clothes off and put them on? Your ivory suit is nice but..."

16

"Right," she whispered, hesitated for another moment, then bent down, pulling at snaps and buttons. "Ivory suit and a frantic escape through the hot, humid, sticky jungle. Probably not a good combination."

She had the guard's shirt off while Goran tugged at the guard's pants. When the man was down to his skivvies, he tossed the pants over to Calista. "Hurry."

Calista was already contorting in an effort to reach the zipper at the back of her dress. Goran sighed and moved swiftly behind her. "Hold still," he snapped, then lifted his hand and pulled down the zipper. Underneath, Goran was surprised to find himself looking at the beautiful skin revealed when the ivory material of her dress slipped away. And a pink bra. A pretty pink bra. With silver thread shot through it.

Whatever he might have pictured, if Goran had ever bothered to picture Calista without her stiff, prim suit on, it definitely wasn't a sexy lace bra. One that barely covered her pretty nipples. Goran tried, and failed, to pull his eyes away from those breasts.

"Stop it! Focus!" she hissed, and turned so that her back was to him. But that only brought his eyes to her ass. Damn, she had a beautiful ass! And he could see almost all of it because of the tiny, matching panties. Okay, what she had on could never be considered a pair of panties. Not in the traditional sense. The scrap of lace that disappeared into the most glorious ass...his mind blanked while he tried to name the kind of panty she had on. Thong, he thought, feeling as if his mind was barely functioning.

A moment later, she tugged the cargo pants up over those glorious globes, hiding her perfect ass from his view. Damn, he wanted to pull her into his arms and rip those pants off of her! Calista? Damn it, he'd been prepared to disengage himself from their engagement. But now, knowing what this woman wore underneath all of those boring, sensible dresses, he was...intrigued. And so turned on, his body was in actual pain.

That last part was a shock, although it probably shouldn't be. He remembered the first time he'd met Calista. There had been a zing of attraction there, perhaps only on his side. And the kiss! That one kiss should have been a prelude to more! But nothing "more" had happened between himself and his lovely fiancée. She'd given him the signal to stay away too many times.

"Stop staring at me!" she hissed, buttoning the jacket and rolling the sleeves up so that her hands came out.

"You're..."

Calista turned around, shoving her hair back behind her shoulders. Glorious hair! He'd never seen her hair down. It had always been confined in some precise, ice-maiden style.

Calista glared at him. "We don't have time for this! We need to get out of here."

She was right, but it irked him that she was more conscious of their tenuous situation than he was. He was battle hardened while Calista sat in a palace and...! Did whatever it was that princesses did in the palace. She was the sister of one of his best friends! She was the sister to one of his country's strongest allies!

And yet, all he could think of were her nipples behind pink and silver lace!

He was going to hell, Goran thought.

Jerking his mind off of those enticing nipples, he focused on getting out of...wherever they were! "Come on," he told her, then pulled her behind his back. Walking to the door, he leaned his head against the wood, listening.

"I think there are only four guards that come and go. Some of them left about twenty minutes ago, although I don't know if they're just outside of whatever building we're in, or if they have left the area."

He looked down at her over his shoulder, lifting a dark eyebrow. He didn't mean to be cynical, but how the hell did she...?

Calista noticed his dubious gaze and rolled her eyes. "While *you* were sleeping," she scoffed, her tone almost accusatory, "I was listening and counting voices and boot footfalls. At times, there were more guards. But they come and go. Some are relatively big men."

He nodded, not bothering to speak out loud as he once again pressed his ear to the wood.

"Earlier, I heard something that made me think that they were sitting at a table. Next room over," she told him, then paused, waiting while he listened. But Calista didn't wait long. "From what I could hear, there are only two rooms in the building. But I think we're higher up than the ground. Not sure what country though. I've heard several different languages, including some that I didn't recognize."

Again, Goran nodded, still listening through the door. "I don't hear anything now."

Calista shifted slightly, then looked down at her shoes. "I can't run in these. I'll break an ankle," she whispered.

Goran looked down as well, then smiled. When he lifted his eyes back up, she was glaring at him and he couldn't stop the chuckle. "I agree with you there. We'll figure something out."

Opening the door, he carefully peered down the hallway. "It's empty," he whispered to her, reaching out as if to take her hand.

Calista smacked it away. "I'm fine," she snapped to him. "I can take care of myself."

Goran looked back at her, his eyes narrowing slightly. He took in her determined expression and relented. "Fine. But..."

"Don't you dare tell me to keep quiet!"

Again, Goran took in her ferocious expression as well as her tense body language. Her pretty hands were fisted at her sides and she looked as if she might try to take him down! How cute, he thought with a shake of his head.

"Stay behind me," he said, instead of saying something that might release those fists towards his head. He'd save that for later, he thought, relishing the idea. His beautiful, always-diplomatic, iceberg fiancée definitely had hidden depths!

He liked that!

Listening carefully, Goran moved slowly down the hallway, pressing his back against the rough wall of the building. He wasn't even sure what kind of a building this was, but he could see the canopy of what he suspected was a jungle area through one of the windows ahead. There were also the sounds of birds and insects chirping away. As he moved down the short hallway, his mind was alert to several sounds but also trying to "feel" the space to determine if there was human occupancy.

When he glanced back, Goran was impressed to notice that Calista was also pressing her back against the wall, her eyes alert as she tried to make herself into the smallest target possible just in case there was someone waiting around the corner with a weapon.

At the doorway to the second room, Goran put his hand out to Calista, his fingers colliding with soft flesh and he heard a soft hiss, but nothing else. Something warned him that he was touching Calista's breast. It had been an accident, but that didn't stop his mind from briefly focusing on the soft fullness before he reminded himself to pull his hand away.

He heard a growl behind him and grinned. If this weren't such a dire situation, he might actually be enjoying himself.

When he peered around the corner of the doorway, Goran discovered that the room was empty. Still alert, he looked around and...weapons! There was a whole wall of weapons! He glanced back at Calista, but he still didn't speak. Both of them moved carefully into the room and looked around. It was a kitchen-like area with a refrigerator and rough shelves, fully stocked with food supplies and a large water tank. On the other wall, there were two narrow cots, which warned him that there was usually more than one guard here.

There were no closets, so he relaxed slightly, nodding to Calista that it was safe to talk.

"Looks like someone might be coming back," Calista said, coming to the same conclusion that he had.

He might have replied, but he was distracted by Calista as she walked over to one of the beds. She found another pair of boots and turned to him. "These are larger. Why don't we trade?" she offered.

Immediately, he nodded and sat down in one of the chairs, unlacing the boots. "See if you can find more of those zip ties. We need to tie up the guard in the other room so that he doesn't present a problem while we're dealing with the next one to arrive, or worse, a full shift change."

Calista dropped the boots and started sifting through the shelves. Securing the other guard was a higher priority at the moment. Seconds later, she lifted a plastic container filled with the zip ties. "This isn't an amateur operation," she stated, glancing at him as she pulled several of the zip ties out of the container. "I'm going to secure the guy in the back room before he wakes up. I'll be right back."

"Calista...no, don't...!" But she was already gone. Quickly, Goran finished tying the boots, which were bigger and much more comfortable, then hurried down the hallway, only to discover that Calista had finished securing the still-unconscious guard with two zip ties on his arms and ankles. She'd also secured him to one of the wooden support beams, keeping the guy from being able to move around the room.

"Good job," he replied, impressed and completely turned on!

Calista shook her head at his praise. "I tied a guy up, Goran. Don't be impressed." She walked out of the room and called out over her shoulder, "Yet!"

Goran's head swiveled to her, watching her sashay down the rough hallway in the oversized cargo pants and tee-shirt that she'd knotted at her waist. She didn't have shoes on yet, having flipped her heels off when she'd spotted the other boots. Gone was the pristine ice princess and in her place was a gorgeous, courageous, stunning woman ready to tackle the world! Damn, she looked hot!

Calista walked back into the "kitchen" area, trying to keep her eyes off of Goran. He'd flipped that guard over without even breaking a sweat! Calista didn't care for how much she'd liked that. But the action had called to her baser feminine instincts.

Goran should look ridiculous in the pressed slacks, filthy and torn dress shirt and combat boots, but...she had to admit that the man looked amazingly virile and...hot. Just incredibly hot!

Forcing her mind to focus on survival and not on the man's impressively tight ass, Calista surveyed the supplies that were neatly stacked and stored around the small shack. There were plenty of weapons, food and water, which meant that someone had planned to keep her and Goran here for a while. Unfortunately, Goran walked back into the small room, his size taking up a significant portion of the space and causing her mind to zip right back to admiring the man instead of concentrating on getting out of this pickle. Stepping back, she continued to survey the area because...because if she looked at Goran, her mind fizzled! The dress shirt might be dirty and torn, but the top few buttons were undone at the neck and Calista desperately wanted to run her fingers over his warm skin.

Now what was that all about? Why was she suddenly attracted to the man who had bored her nearly to tears a mere...how long had they been here?

"How long do you think we've been gone?" she asked, turning to grab a glass. She sniffed it, trying to determine if it was clean.

"I don't know," he replied, grabbing a glass as well, then pouring himself some water, downing the entire amount in mere seconds. He then poured another glass, but handed it to her. "You're probably more dehydrated than you think," he said as an explanation.

Calista smiled slightly, putting down the glass she was holding and taking the glass of water he offered. She was very careful to not touch the man, confused about her recent reactions. It didn't make any sense that she could hate the man one day and be unable to take her eyes off of his butt the next!

Realizing that she was staring at his shoulders...again...Calista turned away, mentally shaking her head. "There's a radio over there," she told him, nodding to the corner where a military grade radio sat, silent at the moment.

"Good. At least we know how they're communicating." He looked over at the beds, then the stash of weapons. "There's another problem."

She finished the water and set the glass down, surprised at how good the water tasted. She really had been thirsty! "Just one other problem?" she asked, feeling like laughing.

He chuckled, shrugging one shoulder. "Okay, we have numerous problems. But the one that comes to mind at the moment is that we're in a tree house."

Calista stared up at Goran, trying to figure out what he was talking about. "A tree house?"

"Yeah," he sighed, looping a finger through his belt at his hip. "We're pretty high up in the trees."

"Oh." She looked around. Sure enough, the only thing she could see through the windows were the tree tops. When she paused to peer over the edge of the "window", Calista discovered that the ground was very far beneath them. "Well, silver lining," she replied with a bright smile, "at least there are screens over the windows to keep the bugs out!"

Goran stared at her with that same odd look she'd seen on his face earlier. She didn't understand what it meant, but it caused her heart to race in a crazy way. What was going on?! These strange sensations were not welcome! Not anymore!

Once again, she forced her mind to focus on the present. "So...if we're so high up, how did we get in here?"

"There's a trap door in the floor over there," he said, his thumb jerking to a point behind him. "I guess the next shift of guards has the exit ladder."

Calista nodded, her eyes searching for and finding the small handle, indicating a square part of the floor that opened up. "That's going to be a challenge, then."

"Probably," he replied.

Calista stood there, not sure what to say. She felt...strange. Normally, her life was so planned out, so orchestrated, that she rarely had time to "wing it". But in this situation, there were no plans, no one telling her to go to the right or left or who's hand she needed to shake and greet and...whatever! A tightness built in her throat as her thoughts spun.

"Okay!" she replied, forcing her mind to stop sliding down the slippery slope towards a full out melt down. "So...what do you think our next step should be?"

Goran understood that Calista was trying to be brave. The lust that her tough demeanor had provoked earlier evolved and a strange, tender sensation entered his chest. He didn't understand what he was feeling, but he knew that she was scared. Moving forward, he took her into his arms.

He suddenly realized how small she was. When she was in heels, Calista came up to his chin. But now that she was in a pair of tough, thick soled boots, the top of her head barely came up to the top of his chest. "It's going to be okay, Calista," he assured her.

For a long moment, she stood stiffly in his arms, neither accepting nor rejecting his comfort. Goran didn't relent. He continued to hold her, running his hand up and down her back. He might not fully understand this tough, beautiful, vulnerable woman, but he was starting to. And this fear, it was deep and hard for her to accept. He'd been around combat hardened soldiers and knew that even they sometimes panicked. Calista was a princess, literally. She was protected at every moment of her day.

He closed his eyes, trying to control his body when she relaxed, leaning into him as she finally accepted his reassurance. It was hard, because her body was soft and perfect and amazing! He wanted to lift her up and kiss her. He wanted to make love to her on one of those ridiculously small cots! He wanted...to make her feel better in any way he could. The fear in those beautiful, dark eyes tore at him!

"Here's my plan," he said softly, burying his nose in her hair. He realized that her hair felt like satin as it draped over his arm and he moved his hand into the dark tresses, needing a longer touch. "That radio over there is going to start spouting information pretty soon. Whoever is at the other end of that radio is counting on the guard tied up in the other room to speak, so we need to talk to that man and get a sense for the cadence of his voice. Maybe he can shed a small bit of understanding for what's going on here."

"You mean, we're going to try and understand why we were kidnapped?" she asked.

"Yes," he confirmed.

"Isn't it to get information out of you?"

He shrugged noncommittally. "That's possible. But I also know how important you are to your brother. As soon as Astir hears of your kidnapping, he'll be crazy with worry."

Calista's eyes widened and he wondered if her lashes had always been that long. That's when he saw the bruise. Her skin was a creamy tan, but there was a darker shade right along her jawline.

"When did this happen?" he demanded, fury coiling inside of him as the tips of his fingers ran along the skin covering that dark spot.

Calista turned her head away, obviously not wanting him to see the bruise. "I'm fine, Goran," she assured him.

He captured her chin between his thumb and forefinger, lifting her head so that he could see the bruise more clearly. "You're not fine!" he growled. "Who hit you?"

"Goran, I don't think that..."

"Calista," he growled, pulling her in closer, glaring down at her now. "You're going to tell me who did this to you."

"I don't know!" she cried out finally. "I don't know, okay? They drugged both of us with something and, whatever it was, started to wear off. Some guy came by in a ski cap and just...knocked me out!"

There was a long pause as he fought to control his rage. Someone had hit his woman! He wanted to find the bastard and pound him into a pulp! "Why didn't you tell me this?"

"Because...because I'd like to be seen as a capable partner in this debacle, okay? Because I've already failed you a moment ago when you recognized that I was starting to panic! I don't want you to..."

He waited for her to continue, but when she merely bit her lip and shrugged as if she didn't want to finish her sentence, he touched her cheek again, prompting her to complete her thought. To be honest with him. "To what?"

She sighed and pulled out of his arms, running her fingers through her hair with frustration. "Look, we already know that we're not compatible."

He'd come to that conclusion before, but things had changed. This kidnapping...it had definitely changed his perception of the real woman behind the royal façade. "We're not?"

"No," she replied, adding a glare for emphasis. "Right before...that blast...whatever that was, I was about to tell you that we should end the engagement. You and I just...we're not right for each other."

"We're not?" he asked, crossing his arms over his chest and leaning a hip against the "kitchen" counter, looking as if he were having a casual conversation instead of being stranded in the middle of a jungle in some foreign country having a conversation with his potentially-soon-to-be-ex-fiancée. "Do tell!"

Calista groaned in frustration. "We don't even like each other, Goran!" she snapped. "You're just..." she let her eyes drift over his arms and shoulders now, pausing. He was built! Seriously built! She hadn't ever seen him without a jacket on, immaculately dressed. But now...holy cow! "Where did all of those muscles come from?"

The startled look in his eyes warned her that her comment about his physique wasn't what he'd been expecting. "My muscles?" he repeated, then released a burst of laughter. "You were going to break up with me because...?"

"No!" she snapped, interrupting him and waving a hand in the air. She sighed, huffing a bit. "I wasn't going to break up with you because I thought you were soft. I was going to break things off between us because you are boring, Goran!" she burst out on a rush of words. "You are boring! Everything we talk about is just...boring!" She ran her fingers through her hair again, pacing around but there wasn't much space in the room so her pacing became a mere circle. "Dear heaven, Goran, every conversation we have with each other is about policy decisions and economic problems! You only need me to show up by your side when there's some sort of public appearance where you need a female to soften your image!"

"Soften my image? You just said that you thought I was soft, without muscles."

24

That reminder caused her eyes to drop once again, surveying his body. "Well, I was...uh...wrong about that." She waved her hand in the air, indicating all of him and turned away. But not before he caught the slight blush tinging her lovely complexion. "You're muscular enough."

He chuckled. "I'm relieved." He pushed away from the counter, moving towards her. "Now tell me again why you were going to end our engagement?"

Calista rolled her eyes. "Don't even try to pretend that you weren't thinking about doing that as well! I saw the look of boredom and disappointment in your eyes. It was there every time you looked at me."

He didn't answer for a long moment, then he tilted his head slightly. "I was...concerned."

"About?"

"About our compatibility."

She snorted and it was a very un-princess-like sound. "You thought I was boring."

He sighed. "Calista..."

She lifted a hand, stopping his explanation. "Don't bother, Goran. We both know that we don't really like each other. You need someone who is..." she looked out the window, mentally groaning. "You need a woman who is happy to be arm candy. I've tried." She blinked back the tears. "I tried very hard to be silent and appear obedient. But I hate it. I hate sitting on the sidelines, listening to what everyone else is thinking and doing and considering." She straightened up, her shoulders flexing, trying to shake off the sudden sick feeling in her stomach. She tried for composure, straightening in the overly large tee-shirt and cargo pants. "I want there to be more to life than simply sitting behind you or walking beside you, being the quiet wife and mother to your children."

"Why would you think that I..."

He was interrupted by a groan coming from the other room. Both of them froze, their eyes clashing with one another.

"I'll go check on him," Goran announced.

"No!" she blurted out, lifting a hand to stop him. "He might talk to me more openly than you."

"Why do you think that?"

Calista shrugged, smiling brightly and with a sudden twinkle of mischief in her eyes. "Because men usually like to brag to me about whatever stupid ideas they have in their mind. I can't tell you how many dinners I've sat through where one diplomat, general or very important person decided to regale me with their latest glorious tale of how impressive they are. And as a representative of my family, I had to endure every one of their stories with a smile on my face and my legs crossed at the ankle." She stepped forward, her grin widening. "Trust me, I've got this."

Neville smiled as he read the news. The Sheik of Skyla was kidnapped along with Princess Calista of Silar. Brilliant! Ned Afrehoster had been a good investment after all! The Silarian government was frantically searching for Princess Calista and the Skyla government was working overtime trying to hide their leader's kidnapping! Absolutely brilliant!

No one was watching the small town in the north of Skyla. It was very close to the border of Silar, so the mining equipment was moving into position during the night hours. It would take two or three days for Neville's people to get everything adequately hidden and another few days to start operations.

He lifted his phone and made a call. "Excellent plan," he said when Ned answered the call. "Give me updates every day. Move up the schedule. I want everything hidden and digging operations started within the next four days instead of a week."

He ended the call, not bothering to wait for Afrehoster's reply. The man would get the work done, or Neville would take care of him the same way he'd taken care of the previous idiots who had failed him over the years.

"Where's my sister?!"

Astir stopped in the doorway, facing a furious woman. "She is…"

Princess Ayla del Taran narrowed her eyes at her older brother. "Don't you dare lie to me. She's not off somewhere with that dud she is engaged to marry. She's not hiding out somewhere, trying to get to know the man. I know for a fact that Calista was going to break up with Sheik Goran after yesterday's official visit."

Astir wasn't sure if he wanted to laugh at his baby sister describing Sheik Goran el Istara as a "dud", furious at the revelation that Calista was going to break things off with a man Astir considered to be a good friend, or jealous that Ayla and Calista obviously had a closer relationship with each other than he had with either of them.

Thankfully, a soothing hand moved over his arm and Astir looked down at Rachel. His wife was…everything, he thought. She soothed him and inflamed him. At just her soft touch, he wanted to pull her into his arms and once again thank her for coming into his life and giving him such joy, as well as toss her over his shoulder and carry her back to their bed so that he could make love to her all over again. The soft roundness of her belly where their child grew only aroused him even more!

Her knowing smile told him that Rachel knew exactly where his mind had gone.

With a sigh, he turned back to Ayla who was still standing in the salon, her tiny hands fisted against her sides and her dark, lovely eyes glaring daggers at him. "Lovely"? When had his tiny, always energetic, always bouncing baby sister turned into such a beautiful woman? And breasts! Uncomfortably, Astir realized that, at some point, his baby sister had grown into an actual woman! She was just a child! How could she have breasts?!

Another touch, this time Rachel laced her fingers through his, and Astir sighed, rubbing his forehead as he tried to concentrate on the current crisis. He could deal with Ayla's inappropriate aging another time. She was frightened now and he needed to reassure her that everything would be okay.

"Ayla, Calista is fine. She's just..."

Ayla tsked with annoyance, slicing her hand through the air to silence him. He almost laughed since that was a gesture that he'd performed several times over the years. Now he knew how annoying it was.

"Don't you dare try to patronize me, Astir. Calista is not fine. She hasn't answered my text messages or answered my calls. The only reason she wouldn't respond is if she *couldn't* respond. So I know that something is wrong." She stepped forward, her dark, almond shaped eyes morphing from anger to pleading. "Astir, just tell me what's going on. I know that you still consider me to be a child. But I'm not. I can handle the truth. What I can't handle is not knowing. My imagination has gone crazy, picturing all the horrific possibilities." Her soft, full lips cringed slightly into a silly grimace before she smoothed her features back to normal. "Trust me, you don't want to be inside my head. It's become a pretty gruesome place." She took yet another step forward. "Just tell me what you know and stop trying to protect me. I'm tougher than you think."

Astir stared at her, stunned all over again. She'd grown breasts and developed into quite a little force of nature.

He almost laughed again when he realized how patronizing his thoughts were. Smoothing his astonishment away, he tightened his fingers around Rachel's briefly, then moved forward, gestured with his hand to the chairs, indicating that they should all sit down.

He paused only long enough to accept the crystal glass of scotch from a servant. "Could you give us some privacy, please?"

The servants standing against the walls immediately moved out of the room and Astir paused, waiting for his body guards to give him the signal that the room was clear.

Only then did he turn to Ayla.

"I'm sorry for keeping you out of the loop. I should have come to you and explained as soon as I had any information."

Ayla immediately waved his apology away. "You're under a great deal of pressure, Astir. I know this. I try to keep out of your way because I know that you don't have much free time." Her eyes turned shiny as tears threatened, but she rallied, straightening her shoulders and leaning forward slightly. "Just tell me what's going on."

Astir sighed. "We don't know," he told her and continued quickly when Ayla's eyes widened. "We know that Goran and Calista were kidnapped at some point between Goran's last speech and the airport, where they were both scheduled to travel home. What we don't know is who took them, or why."

"Do you have any theories?" she asked, her eyes pleading now and Astir noticed that her hands were clenched together so tightly that her knuckles were white with the strain.

"We have a few, but..." he rubbed his forehead. "They just don't make sense. And once my security team looks into one possibility, they dismiss it because the evidence doesn't back it up." He looked her directly in the eyes as he said, "We're going to get Calista back, Ayla. And I promise that I'll keep you informed in the future."

She smiled slightly, but the warmth didn't reach her eyes as she said, "Thank you for that." She stood up then. Ayla straightened her shoulders and took a slow, deep breath, then nodded firmly. "I'm not a baby anymore. I can handle real life."

And with that, she walked forward and threw her arms around Astir, hugging him tightly. After brushing a brief kiss to his cheek, she straightened out once again, smoothed a hand down over her stomach to ease the non-existent wrinkles out of her dress and walked to the door. Even as he watched, Ayla paused, with one hand on the doorknob, took in a slow, deep breath, then lifted her chin, pasted a calm smile to her features and opened the door.

When they were alone again, Rachel said what he was feeling. "Wow!"

Astir agreed. Ayla had become a stunningly beautiful woman. The strong-willed, stubborn, energetic child had somehow grown up without him noticing!

Chapter 4

Goran watched Calista as she walked down the short, rough-plywood hallway. She looked beautiful and confident, the ill-fitting clothing not diminishing her beauty in any way. She even managed to walk like a princess despite the boots that clunked slightly against the rough wood floors. Damn, she was beautiful! How had he missed her demeanor? How had he completely misconstrued that façade for who she was as a person?

When she stopped in the doorway, he watched with fascination as she paused, curved her shoulders forward slightly, bowed her head and... sniffed? What the hell?

As she entered the room, instead of her confident stride, she stepped through the door hesitantly, pausing ever so slightly in the doorway before going fully into the room.

Curious, Goran walked silently down the hallway towards the door, needing to understand what was going on.

There were a few whispered calls to the man as she attempted to wake him up. She wasn't mean about it, barely patting his cheek and swishing her hand away, as if the mere touch of her hand against his skin burned her fingertips.

Or as if she was scared of the guard's reaction. Afraid that he might wake up and grab her arm? But...Calista had secured the man's arms behind his back, then tied him to the wooden beam! What the hell was she playing at?

"Mister!" she hissed, then furtively looked over her shoulder to see if the doorway was still clear. Goran didn't move. He remained in place, listening. "Mister!" she said with more force.

"Huh?" the man grunted and Goran suspected that he'd just woken from unconsciousness. "What the hell?"

29

"Don't move!" she hissed, still crouched down, her arms wrapped around her knees.

"How the hell did you get free? I tied you up myself!"

Calista shushed him. "Don't talk too loudly!" she urged. "Please?"

There was a pregnant pause, then she continued. "What's going on? Why are we here?"

There was some shuffling and Goran knew that the guard was trying to break the restraints, then hissed when the effort tugged on the pinched nerves Goran had used to knock him out. The restraints held, but Goran's fingers touched the stolen pistol that he'd tucked into his belt, ready for anything.

"Don't," she whispered. "You're already hurt. You don't want to further damage your shoulder. And I suspect that we all need to save our energy for when...well, what's going on? I don't understand!"

"You're supposed to be in here, tied up! Not me! What the hell happened?"

Calista shrugged her slender shoulders, her whole figure looking more delicate because of the oversized clothing. "I don't know! I don't know why I'm here or why you're here! I don't even know where here is!"

"Get me out of these damn restraints, bitch! Then I'll show you what the hell is going on!"

Calista moved over to the man, shifting carefully, shuffling in her oversized boots. She reached behind the man, but kept herself far away from him. She tugged, then jerked quickly back, scooting quickly away.

"I can't get them undone! What should I do?"

"Break the damn ties, you stupid bitch!"

"Not if you're going to speak to me like that!" she shot back at him and Goran wondered why she sounded so hoity toity now. He'd never heard her use that tone before but...hell, it was convincing. Even he thought she sounded extra princessy now.

There was a deep, heavy sigh, then the bound guard shifted around slightly. He couldn't move very far because Calista had done a great job of restraining him.

"I'm sorry," the man replied. "If you could just...get these plastic ties off of my wrists, then I can do the rest."

Calista moved again, but once more, she jerked backwards. "Ouch!" she hissed. "I broke a nail!"

"Honey, if you don't get me out of these restraints, I'm going to break more than just a nail!"

Calista huffed and he watched as she moved to the other side of the room, obviously not helping the man anymore. Once more, she curled her arms around her legs, seeming to try and become smaller and more nonthreatening.

"You brought me here. Get yourself out of those ties!"

"You stupid..."

"Call me a bitch again and I'll leave! I'll go eat all of that food and... and you'll have nothing until that other guy comes back!"

"The other...!" The man huffed a bit, as if trying to regain a measure of his patience. "Tell me that the stupid bastard you are engaged to is still around."

Calista shrugged. "I don't know exactly where he is." That was the truth, he thought. She knew that Goran was still in the shack but the "exactly" gave her that small bit of honesty that helped her sell the routine.

Suddenly, Goran understood what she was doing. And he thought she was amazing! It was one of the best interrogation techniques! Damn, she was beautiful, sexy, and brilliant!

There was a long silence and Goran settled in to wait. Sure enough, after only a few minutes of silence, the bound guard started talking.

"It isn't you that we're after, lady."

"Oh," she replied, her voice soft and tentative. "Okay."

"It's your boyfriend."

Nothing.

"We aren't going to hurt either of you." The man laughed, but there wasn't much amusement in his voice. "We're not idiots. No way are we going to hurt either of you. We don't want a death sentence on our heads."

Goran rolled his eyes. Too late, he thought. They'd kidnapped the ruler of Skyla! What the hell did this guy think was going to happen to him and his cohorts when his security team found them? And yes, his security team would find the conspirators. Every last one of them! No way were these idiots going to get away with kidnapping him and Calista and live to prosper from their efforts!

"We just need your boyfriend out of the way for a while. That's it."

There was a suspicious sniff and Goran suspected that Calista was crying now. Or pretending to cry.

"My head hurts," she whispered. "What did you drug me with?"

"Nothing much. Just..." he sighed and there was a small thud. Goran suspected that the bound guard had leaned his head against the wooden wall a bit too heavily. "I think the guy in charge gave your buddy a shot of ketamine." He lifted his head and looked at Calista. "You just got a little tap to the head. Nothing much. Just enough to keep you knocked out for a while."

"Thank you." Goran heard another sniff.

31

Ketamine? He'd been injected with ketamine?! That was a horse tranquilizer! And a date rape drug. Damn them!

"It wasn't a lot. We just needed the big guy out of commission until we could get him here. It obviously wore off if I'm now tied up and he's free."

"He's not here," she confirmed.

"Of course he's not here you stupid...!" The guard stopped his tirade before he said something that might hurt Calista's feelings. For a brief moment, Goran considered walking into the room to punch the guy, teach him a lesson for raising his voice in front of Calista. But she must have anticipated that because she raised her voice loud enough to hear over the man's yelling.

"If you keep on yelling, then Sheik el Istara is going to come in here! Neither of us want that!"

Goran almost laughed but he relaxed his muscles, leaning against the wall once again. Message received, he thought silently. And timely! How had she known that Goran was ready to burst into the room?

"Fine! But seriously, what good are you? You can't even get me out of these ties! How the hell had he tightened the damn things like this? And..." Goran suspected the man was trying to see behind his back. "What did he tie me to?"

"How in the world would I know?"

The man sighed and there was another thud. "Right. I forgot. You're just some stupid bitch who..."

"If you insult me one more time, then I'm..."

He chuckled, interrupting her. "I know. You're going to head back into the kitchen and eat up all the junk food." The guy sighed. "Lady, you're a piece of work!"

"Why did you need him out of the way?"

"Hell if I know!" the guy replied. "I just follow orders. And the person who needs lover boy out of the way was willing to pay a massive amount of money to make that happen."

"But...if His Highness is out of the way for too long, then they'll just declare his advisory council to be in charge. And they advise him on what needs to be done. So...what's the point? I mean, it's not like any laws can be made without His Highness around."

"Like I said," he muttered, "I just follow the money."

Goran knew that the guard didn't know much and he needed a way to get Calista out of the room, but not to blow her cover. There might be other questions that would occur to them and the guard might know that answer.

So he moved quietly over to the second room and started making some noise, hoping the sounds came across as what it would sound like if he were climbing back up through the trap door.

"Calista!" he bellowed, loud enough to be heard for a ways.

He heard a bit of whispering, then Calista slunk out of the room, appearing scared as she cowered slightly, pressing her shoulders against the wall.

As soon as she was out of the guard's line of sight, she pulled the door closed and...transformed back into the cool, confident woman!

"Where the hell were you?" he roared, slapping his hand down against the wooden wall.

Calista smiled, her eyes twinkling with that conspiratorial glimmer that he thought was so hot!

"I'm sorry, Your Highness!" she replied in a relatively loud voice.

Goran was too impressed and he couldn't hold back any longer. He eliminated the two steps that separated them, his arm whipping out to wrap around her waist. A second later, he had her pressed against his body and he was kissing her. Hard!

And even more astounding, Calista was kissing him back. In fact, her arms were wrapped around his shoulders and her surprisingly muscular legs wrapped around his waist and she was kissing him with as much passion and intensity as he was feeling. Swinging her around, he set her down on the counter in order to move his hands more freely.

He jerked her forward, her hips shifting against his lengthening erection as she tilted her head back to deepen the kiss. Again and again, his mouth slashed over hers, his tongue invading the moist heat of her mouth, doing to her lips what he wanted to do to her body! When he felt her fingers in his hair, pulling his head down to hers, he almost lost control. It was only by sheer force of will that he pulled his body back from the brink, his breathing ragged as he slowed the kiss, then pulled away. He stared down at her, unable to stop his hands as they continued to shift and slide against her bottom, her back, her thighs...anywhere he could touch her.

Calista gasped, shivering as his fingers dove into her hair, pulling her head further back as Goran kissed her again. She couldn't get enough of him. A part of her mind told her to stop this insanity, but the other part of her brain warned that if he stopped, she might actually cry! Pulling him closer, she shifted against him, pressing her body closer, needing more of him than might be possible!

The muffled sounds of something thudding finally broke through the haze of lust surrounding both of them, but Calista was furious that Goran was the first to pull away.

"What's wrong?" she whispered. That's when she realized that her fingers were in his hair, pulling on the soft strands. Not just her fingers, but her entire body was tangled with his! Her legs were tight around his waist and her body strained to get closer.

"I think that our prisoner is trying to escape his bonds," Goran explained, his voice a low, rumbling sound that tingled over her skin, sending her nerve endings clamoring for another kiss. Just one more!

"I should go investigate."

Calista stared at him, still trying to understand what he was saying. Investigate? But wouldn't that take his very delectable body away from hers?

She replayed the words in her mind. Then did it again. Straining to comprehend what he was saying. Neither of them moved until another, louder, thud caught their attention.

In that moment, both of them jerked away as if they'd been burned. Calista's breathing was still ragged, but she lifted a trembling hand to cover her mouth. She could feel how swollen her lips were from his kisses, and she tried to hide the fact that she was so affected.

"I'm going to check on him," Goran announced.

"Right," she replied, then waited until he'd walked down the short hallway before she looked around. Suddenly, Calista realized where she was sitting, perched on the very edge of the rough board that was acting as a countertop, and she jumped down, walking as far away from that spot as possible in the small room. Pressing her shoulders back against the thin wood of the wall, she stared at the spot where... what had happened? She'd...kissed...Goran? She'd actually kissed him? And...just yesterday, she'd vowed that she would extricate herself from an engagement with a man who was boring and tedious and...didn't want her!

Hmmm...perhaps that last part wasn't true. Her mind thought back to the pressure of his...well....him, against her body. He wasn't just interested, he was *impressively* interested!

She heard the sound of sharp words, but wasn't sure what Goran was saying to the man tied up in that other room. Regardless, she took the few moments of privacy to pull herself together.

So when Goran stepped out of the room again, she was busy pulling open cabinet doors, pretending to search the contents for...whatever might be helpful, something that might extricate them from this situation.

"He's still secured," Goran announced as soon as he stepped back into the small room. "But I think we should figure out how to get out of here. I doubt that we'll remain safe once the next shift arrives."

"I agree." She turned around, her hands holding two cans of food as she looked at the shelves, the floor, the trap door and...anywhere that wasn't Goran.

"About what happened a moment ago..." he started off.

Darn it! Trust him to be direct about an uncomfortable situation! She shook her head, unwilling to deal with that problem at the moment. "It was a moment of insanity. We were just..." she searched her brain for a viable reason for what had just transpired between them. "Let's just pretend that it didn't happen."

He glared down at her and Calista knew that he wasn't going to "pretend".

"Calista, we should..."

"Sheets!" she gasped, turning away from him.

"Sheets?"

She sort-of glanced at him over her shoulder. "Yes. We could tear the sheets up and use them as a way to get down to the ground. There are two sheets and two blankets." She turned and looked up at him, hope lighting her eyes for the first time since she'd woken up in this miserable situation. "That should be enough to get us down to the ground, right?"

Goran cast a measuring glance over at the small cots, then nodded sharply. "I think you're right," he replied, then moved over to the cots, stripping the sheets and blankets off. "You go through the cabinets and gather up whatever food and water supplies that we can carry." He ripped the pillows up as well, using that material for additional length as he started knotting the sheets and blankets together. "This will definitely be long enough. I'll tie the length to that support beam over there."

Calista hurried through the cabinets, gathering several cans up and dumping them into the pockets of her cargo pants.

"Calista...?"

She understood his tone and her shoulders drooped, but she didn't turn to look at him. "Look, Goran, we both know that we're not very interested in each other. That kiss...it was just a fluke. Just like the time we kissed after my brother's wedding." Calista paused, closing her eyes briefly. "We were..." she opened her eyes and looked through the small window, searching for inspiration. "We were finding comfort in each other's arms during a stressful situation. I understand that." She looked over at him. "I know you're not interested in me. And before we were kidnapped, I was searching for a way to end our engagement. So don't stress about it, okay? Like I said, that kiss was just a fluke. A release of stress. Nothing more. We're still two people who don't really like each other."

He stared at her for such a long time, Calista wondered if he was going to disagree with her statement. She waited, praying that he'd disagree. Praying that he might say that he really did like her, that they just needed to get to know one another better. Perhaps their interactions had been too public oriented and they needed to get to know each other's private personas.

Instead, he nodded sharply. "Right," was his only response. Were the muscles in his jaw a bit tighter? Was there a bit more tension in those surprisingly muscular shoulders?

Again, Calista didn't really know him well enough to be able to differentiate between irritated-Goran and focused-Goran. So instead of trying to figure him out, she moved efficiently through the "cabin" collecting anything that might be useful.

Goran tied the strips of sheets and blankets together, leaving the pillowcases for packing up supplies. But the whole time, he wondered what the hell Calista had meant by her words. He "wasn't interested in her?" How in the world could she think that?

Goran wiped the sweat from his face with the sleeve of his arm. The humidity was so thick, it was like a physical hindrance. He much preferred the dry heat of his desert country, but he knew that others loved the sultry air created by the humid climates. He didn't understand how anyone could enjoy this kind of thick, "wet" air, but he was quickly discovering a lot of issues he didn't understand.

How in the hell could anyone not lust after Calista?

Okay, she came across as a prim ice princess most of the time. But there'd been that one kiss. Now two kisses. Hmm...that last kiss moments ago had been a hell of a lot more than just a kiss. It had been... mind blowing! And if Calista thought that she was going to end their engagement after that experience...!

Goran glanced over at her, noticed the sweat staining her shirt, her dark hair that was cascading down her back...hair that was normally pulled back into a tight style that caused her features to look pinched and strained. Right now, she didn't look pinched or strained. She looked...lovely! Nor was she complaining. Ever since he'd woken up out of the drug induced stupor, Calista hadn't uttered a single complaint. Most the other women of his acquaintance would have been whining, demanding that he do something to get them out of this predicament.

Not Calista! She was working just as hard to find a solution as he was. Damn, he respected her for that! In that moment, she bent over to put something into one of the pillow case bags and...seeing her ass in that manner...! He went from appreciative of her personality to rock hard with lust in record time!

What the hell was it about Calista that made him burn like this? Turning away from the delectable image, he focused on the weapons. Checking them for ammunition and ensuring that the safety locks were on, he stuffed two of them into the waistband of his slacks, nestled against his back. He flung one of the rifles over his shoulder and was reaching for another when soft, feminine hands reached for it. Turning, he was startled to see Calista flinging the rifle over her shoulder, the strap nestling between her breasts. Lucky strap, he thought, then lifted his eyes to her face.

"Do you know how to use that?" he asked, his body tightening as he looked down at her.

Calista lifted her eyes, challenge simmering in those lovely, dark depths. Goran laughed softly, shaking his head. "You continue to astonish me, love."

"Is that 'rope' going to hold us?"

Goran looked at the sheets and blankets knotted together and nodded. "Yeah, the material hasn't been out here long enough for the humidity to have deteriorated the fabric. We should be good."

Calista nodded as she moved over to the trap door. "What are we going to do about the guy tied up in the other room?"

"Nothing," he replied, hefting the heavy door open. He secured the "rope" to one of the shack supports and gestured for her to move closer to him.

"What do you mean? We have to help him! We can't just leave him here. He'll die!"

Goran put his arms around her, slipping the makeshift rope around her waist. "How about if we figure out how to survive ourselves? If we can make it out of this jungle, then I'll send someone to rescue the guy. Will that work for you?"

Calista nodded, grabbing the rope. "Yes. That's a fair trade." She grinned as she tugged at the rope to ensure that it was strong enough. "You made this loop just for me, didn't you? You're going to lower me down instead of trusting me to shimmy down like a normal person?"

He chuckled, moving behind her as his body tightened once again. "You're my princess, honey," he said and shifted the loop so it was more secure around her. He lowered his head, saying into her ear, "What kind of fiancé would I be if I didn't see to your every comfort?"

Before she could respond, he lifted the rope up and carefully lowered her through the trap door. It took only a few moments to lower her all the way to the ground. When her feet touched the jungle floor, she wiggled herself out of the loop and turned, looking up at him.

Goran pulled the "rope" back up and tied up the two pillow cases filled with supplies, then lowered those down next. As Goran watched from above, Calista efficiently untied the bags and set them off to the side. But not before he got a very good glimpse of her breasts encased in that pink and silver lace. He groaned, and this time, he didn't bother trying to hide his reaction since he was about twenty feet above her.

"Anything else?" she called out, her beautiful face turned to look up at him. She wiped sweat from her brow, then took her booted foot and stepped on the loop, securing the "rope" for him.

"I think that's all that is salvageable," he called down. There was a bit of thumping from the other room and Goran knew that the guard had finally understood what they were doing and was trying to break free from his restraints. But his sexy, adorable fiancée was damn good at securing wrists and ankles. The other guy wasn't going anywhere.

Goran wrapped his hands around the rope held taught by her body weight, trapping the rope between his feet as he shimmied down the "rope". He idly wondered if he would be as good at securing more delicate wrists. He'd tried that sort of experience before when one of his mistresses had asked him to tie her up, but he hadn't been as into it as she had been. But the idea of a bound Calista, a time when he would have complete control over her incredible body...? The idea was much more appealing than he would have thought possible.

"Focus on getting out of this situation," he grumbled as he lowered himself down to the ground.

As soon as he turned around, Calista was there and he wrapped an arm around her waist, holding her close to him. "Thanks for keeping the rope steady," he murmured, brushing his lips over her mouth.

Unfortunately, she pulled back, blinking those long, dark lashes up at him. However, he could see the pulse pounding rapidly against the tender skin at the base of her neck. She was just as affected as he was, he thought with approval.

"Let's go," he grumbled.

"Wait!" she called out.

Goran stopped and turned back to her. "What? Do you...?"

He looked in the direction she was pointing and saw it. "A ladder!" he groaned. "Right!"

"We should climb back up and cut the rope down, right?" she suggested. "I mean, if someone comes to check on us, to make sure that the other guard is still okay, then it would be better if they didn't immediately see the rope hanging down."

He nodded sharply. "You're right. A rope like that is a dead giveaway that someone escaped. And the most likely culprits would be us, the two people they are trying to keep restrained."

"I'll bring it over," she told him, already walking towards the tall ladder.

"I've got..." he started to say, thinking that he didn't want her to hurt herself by bringing over the heavy ladder. But she simply lifted the ladder up, carrying it over, then leaning it carefully against the opening through which they'd just descended.

"All set." She then stepped back, a look of determination in those eyes that he was really coming to admire and...more? Yes, there was a hell of a lot more to Calista than he'd originally thought. Gone was the prim little ice princess and in her place was a strong, determined woman who was more than equal to the task of getting them out of this place!

With speed, he climbed the ladder and, with her shoe-knife, cut away the sheets and blankets, letting everything fall to the ground. When he was standing on the ground once more, she was already gathering up the "rope".

"I'll hide this in the jungle so that it's not visible."

"Be careful of the spiders," he called out. He waited but Calista only hesitated for a brief moment before she continued walking into the lush green jungle. She went about ten steps, then tossed the "rope" on the ground, using her "new" heavy boots to scrape enough of the underbrush over the sheets to hide it from casual viewers.

"I'm going to hide the ladder," he called out. He was carrying the ladder through several of the trees when he heard the sound.

Glancing over at Calista, he realized that she'd heard it too. They both froze for a precious second, but a brief moment later, he saw her rushing over the trampled ground towards him. She took a moment to bend over and grab the two bags of supplies while Goran tossed the ladder into the jungle. He didn't bother to cover it up because there wasn't time. The engine was getting louder and they needed to find cover.

"Get down," he told her, but Calista was already by his side, bending down low so that the jungle foliage hid them from view.

Goran reached behind himself, pulling out one of the pistols. They both had the rifles slung over their bodies, but a pistol was usually more accurate and more maneuverable in close combat like this.

Thinking quickly, Goran watched as two guards stepped out of the Jeep. They weren't paying much attention to their surroundings, which was a major failure in any sort of combat situation, he thought. But worse, they were joking around, slapping each other on the backs and laughing about their success. He made note of everything that these guards did wrong, needing to inform his own military commanders so that lessons could be learned.

"Tell me again how much we're making on this insane mission?" the second man called out.

"Shut up and get the ladder, you freak!" another man called out.

The first man laughed, walking towards the space where the ladder had previously been leaning against the edge of the tree. "Where the hell did you put it after we left here the last time?"

The second man was pulling out a metal box, probably filled with more supplies, maybe even ammunition based on the strength of the steel box, but he looked over at the first guy, tilting his head towards the base of the tree. "It's right there, you moron."

Americans? Calista mouthed.

Goran listened for another moment, then shook his head. "No," he mouthed right back. But he struggled to place the accent. It wasn't quite American. At least not any American accent he'd ever heard of. Nor was it British or Irish. The accent definitely wasn't Scottish or Welsh. There was no lilting quality to their vowels. Canadian? He considered that possibility for a long moment, then discarded it.

He suspected that these men were from all over the world, not pledging allegiance to any particular country. They were mercenaries, to be sure, but trying to figure out their nationality would be pointless. They weren't associated with a particular country. Mercenaries lost their accents through time and effort, not wanting to be attributed to any specific region for fear of their competition or enemies, two different species, to dig into their past and discover a weakness. The lack of a specific accent also protected their families, if they had any. If one couldn't find a mercenary's loved ones, it was harder to find their Achilles heel.

"The ladder isn't here!" the other guy called out, frustrated but becoming more alert, his head swiveling around as if searching the area for a threat. "You said you put it at the base of the tree?"

The other man set the heavy box down, becoming more alert as well. "What the hell?" he muttered, his voice muted as he swung the rifle from his back so that it was covering the front of him.

Both men were now looking around, their eyes searching the foliage for threats. Calista and Goran automatically crouched lower, even though Goran's automatic reaction was to confront instead of hide. He had to protect Calista now. He couldn't put her in danger by confronting the other men, even though he was fairly certain that he could take both of them down without a bullet being fired.

"I'm going to the other side," she whispered in an almost silent voice. Obviously, she was aware of how far voices carried.

Before Goran could stop her, she settled low near the ground and moved on her hands and knees, oblivious or just unconcerned with the potential snakes, spiders, or other creepy crawly things that might intersect with her path.

Unfortunately, she was already too far away for him to tell her to stop. He couldn't raise his voice loud enough to reach her for fear that he'd be overheard and discovered. That was not the way to stage an attack, he mentally muttered.

But only thirty seconds later, he saw her a good distance away, almost on the other side of the small clearing. He'd figure out how she'd gotten so far in such a short period of time – but he'd figure that out later. Right now, he needed to take care of the two men who were now on high alert, their heads and eyes swiveling around in search of the threat.

Goran looked through the leaves at her and knew...he just knew what she was going to do. He couldn't stop her, and in the back of his mind, he knew that her plan was pretty damn good. He still didn't like it. The idea of her being in danger, no matter how slight, made him crazy.

So when she nodded at him, he was ready.

Calista stood up and looked around, acting as if she were lost.

"Oh, thank heaven's you're here!" she called out. "I was so worried that some of the horrible men who tried to hurt me earlier would come by." She stepped out from the trees, pushing the thick leaves away as if they might somehow poison her. The reality was that there were some trees in this area of the world that truly could harm her. And right now, Goran wasn't going to assume that she didn't know the difference. Not anymore. He was quickly discovering that Calista was much more intelligent than he'd ever given her credit for.

The first guy did a quick double take, his rifle coming up but not pointing at Calista. "How the hell did you get down here?" he demanded, his body tight with tension.

Calista's "dumb" act continued as she widened her eyes. "I don't really know," she lied. "I just...I think I sort of woke up over here in the dirt. Thankfully, it doesn't get too cold here at night."

The second man stepped forward, his attention completely focused on Calista. Stupid move, Goran replied as he stealthily moved towards him. Calista, damn her, moved out of the jungle, heading towards the first guy. He wanted to yell at her to stay away, to tell her that he could handle both men without any problem. But there was no way to tell her that without alerting the other men to his presence.

41

The thick, wet earth muffled the sound of his steps as he crept closer and closer. Calista continued to tell both men how grateful she was that they'd finally arrived, that she was thirsty for water, that she was hungry and "Ewww! How many spiders were there in this horrible place!" she cried out, jumping around as if a monster sized spider was about to attack. That last part allowed him to move faster, but it also allowed her to shift her body closer and closer to the second guy.

Seconds later, Goran had his arm wrapped around the first guy and, moments later, the lack of oxygen to his brain caused him to tumble to the ground. When Goran looked up, ready to help Calista with her guy, he watched in amazement as, while the guard was distracted by Goran's movements, she grabbed the man's wrist, rammed her elbow into his solar plexus, then followed that up by flipping the man over her shoulder, using her back for leverage. A fraction of a second later, Calista had the man on the ground, his face planted in the dirt with his arm pulled unnaturally behind his back and his fingers twisted into a painful movement.

"Don't move, and I won't dislocate your shoulder!" she hissed into the man's ear, her knee pressing him down. The man wasn't going any-where, not with her hold on him like that. Goran ran over and tied the man's hands behind his back using the plastic zip ties they'd grabbed from the shack. He tied the man's ankles as well, then used another plastic zip tie to attach him to one of the trees, ignoring the man's curses as he tried to break free from the restraints.

The other man was easier to tie up since he was still unconscious.

The entire event took less than three minutes. When both guards were restrained, Calista slapped her hands together, trying to brush off some of the dirt. When Goran looked over at her to ensure that she was okay, he noticed that she was filthy, covered in mud and sweat, and yet, she looked even more beautiful than he'd ever seen her.

Calista watched as Goran dragged the unconscious guard over to one of the trees, wishing that she had a comb. Or just some water to wash her face and hands. She must look filthy, but there wasn't much she could do about it. She was just...a mess.

And yet, she couldn't believe how sexy Goran looked at this moment. Watching him move towards the guards, the agile movements of his arms and hands as he brought the other man down. She felt her heart race and it had nothing to do with her own flipping of the guard to the ground. It was all because she was so turned on by Goran's manly endeavors.

Just a few days ago, she'd thought he was just a politician! Wow, she'd been so wrong! The man had hidden his muscles underneath those elegant suits. And he'd hidden his athletic capabilities as well! Goodness, she'd never thought of herself as someone who was enamored of men who could fight, but here she was, literally vibrating with sexual awareness simply because Goran had taken an armed guard out of commission with his bare hands. Plus, he hadn't killed the guy! Bonus, she thought.

"Good job," she called out to him, lifting her eyes up to his as he approached.

"You're so hot!" he whispered as one of those muscular arms whipped around her waist, pulling her against his hard body. "Don't ever put yourself in danger like that again." And then he was kissing her. This wasn't a small brush of his lips against hers either. This was hard, demanding, sultry and erotic. She felt this kiss all the way down to her toes.

Unfortunately, they weren't out of danger yet and he pulled back before she was satisfied with the kiss. As if that could happen, she scoffed! Calista wondered if she'd ever be satisfied with his kisses! Damn, he made her feel incredibly good!

Why hadn't he kissed her like this over the past year? Why hadn't he held her like this? Why hadn't she discovered that he was strong and capable – and not just a pretty face?

All questions she'd ask herself at a later time.

"We need to get out of here," she whispered against his lips.

"You're right," he replied, then smiled. "And now we don't have to walk out of here." He lifted his free hand, dangling a set of keys in his fingers. "Ready to go?"

She laughed, delighted with the man and lifting up onto her toes to give him one more kiss, ignoring the grumbling and cursing of the two men tied up to trees on opposite sides of the small clearing.

"Ready," she muttered, her mind a bit flustered by his strong arm around her waist as well as the hardness pressing against her. She was confused and so turned on she could barely think straight. That was a danger when they were fleeing for her life, so she pulled out of his arms. "Want me to drive?" she asked, then laughed when he gave her a "get real" look as he slipped into the driver's seat. She pulled open the passenger door and stepped inside, then slammed the door shut just as the engine roared to live.

"You don't think any animals will come in to hurt those men, do you?" she asked, looking worriedly at the men who were glaring daggers at them from their positions in the dirt.

His response was a low, throaty chuckle as he put the Jeep in gear.

"You're such a Pollyanna!"

She rolled her eyes and shifted in the passenger seat so that she was looking forward. "Right, that coming from a G.I. Joe!"

He laughed again, then spun the steering wheel to turn the Jeep around so they could head out of the small clearing in the same direction the guards had arrived.

While Goran drove, Calista twisted around, searching the Jeep for a map or some other piece of information that would tell them where they were. "We need to figure out what country we're in," she told him, unaware of his perusal of her butt while she sifted through the equipment in the back of the Jeep. Because there weren't any paved roads, the going was rough and she bounced around quite a bit, but Calista was determined to find something that would lead them out of this godforsaken jungle! Finding air conditioning was her goal.

"Aha!" she called out, then turned back around, sliding into the passenger seat as she held up a laminated map triumphantly. "We're in..." she searched the map, looking for clues. "Costa Rica?" she gasped, then turned to look at Goran. "We were held captive in one of the happiest countries in the world?"

"Costa Rica is the happiest place?"

She shrugged, turning her attention back to the map. "According to several surveys I've read. Although, I don't know if the residents of Costa Rica are happier because they don't have a lot of competition or if there's something more to the happy factor that other populations don't grasp."

For the next hour, they drove through the jungle, both of them scanning the horizon as well as the rear of the vehicle for anything that might be a danger, such as additional guards searching for their missing captives.

"Something just occurred to me," she called out when they suddenly reached a rough, gravel road.

"What's that?"

She put a hand to his arm, stopping him from driving out onto the road. "What if there's a tracking device in this vehicle?" she asked. "I mean, those guards weren't the most trustworthy gentlemen. Whoever kidnapped us has some money. The supplies and the vehicle, not to mention the out of the way place where we were being held, all add up to someone with a lot of money. From the conversations we overheard, I suspect that the guards are all mercenaries, trading their services to the highest bidder. What's to say that the person who developed this plan didn't trust the people they'd hired?"

Goran looked as if he might argue with her initially, but when she finished her explanation, he nodded his head sharply. "Good point." He put the Jeep in park and got out. "I'll search the undercarriage."

"I'll look through the supplies," she told him.

Five minutes later, both of them held a small tracking device in their hands. Looking down at them, Goran shook his head. "Good job!" he told her. "Brilliant thinking!" And he pulled her into his arms again moments before he took both of the tracking devices and tossed them into the woods. "Let's go," he said as they both hopped back into the Jeep.

Two hours later, they came to a paved highway. Goran looked over at her, dark eyebrows raised. "What do you think? Right or left?"

Calista bit her lower lip as she surveyed the highway. "Well, it occurs to me that we really can't..."

"...Be seen in public yet," he finished her thought. "I know. That thought occurred to me as well."

She sighed. "We don't know who was involved in helping those men kidnap us."

"There had to be an inside person helping out."

"Right." She tapped a ragged, filthy fingernail on top of the map. "I know for certain that my brother wasn't involved. We could call him. He could arrange a place where we could hide out until he gets more information."

He thought about that for a long moment, his eyes scanning the highway in both directions. There wasn't a lot to see, since this wasn't a particularly populated portion of the countryside. "I think that would work. But the next question is how are we going to contact him."

Calista shrugged her shoulders. "I'm stumped there too," she replied.

He rubbed the scruffy beard on his jawline, then eyed her warily. "I'm going to propose something and I don't want you to reject the idea until you've thought about it for a long moment."

She looked at him warily. "Okay, what?"

"We need to steal a phone," he told her. "We can't use any of the equipment here in this Jeep, even if we found a phone in those boxes."

She nodded, understanding where he was going. "The phone might be tracked." She sighed and looked around. "Okay, but if we're going to steal something, we have to do it in a place where it won't be missed immediately."

"I suggest we find a tourist area, maybe a resort, where we could blend in a bit more."

She looked down at her filthy clothes, fingernails and skin. "I don't think there are any tourist areas where we could blend in very easily."

He laughed, nodding. "Okay, let's find a place to clean up a bit first.

Let me see the map."

She handed it to him, then leaned over and pointed a grubby finger at one place she'd been considering. "I think this road leads to a waterfall. I'm not sure, but the topography looks familiar."

The sun was high overhead now, indicating that it was around midday. The heat was stifling and, combined with the ever-present humidity, it was unbelievably oppressive. There was a trail of sweat running down the side of Calista's cheek and she wiped it away, but not a single complaint did she utter. The woman was truly amazing!

"Let's try it," he replied, turning at the small space she'd indicated. "Worst case, at least we can clean up a bit." He tilted his head towards the back.

"I'll see if there are any toiletries back here," she replied.

Goran stifled another groan. More torture, he thought. Sure enough, a moment later, she twisted her body and did that butt-wiggling thing again. Damn, she had a mighty fine ass! And even in this sweltering heat, she smelled good! Very good! There was a soft, feminine scent about Calista that...now that they were alone and not surrounded by strangers, he could mentally pause to appreciate.

Was that all that they'd needed over the past several months? A bit of time to get to know each other? No, he thought as he maneuvered the Jeep over the rough, barely-there road. He doubted that simply spending time in a normal setting with Calista would have allowed her, or him, the freedom to really relax and let their true personalities be revealed to one another. She had always seemed so tightly wound, so closed off to him as well as the rest of the world.

"I think I found something!" she called out, then shimmied herself back into the passenger seat. "Ta-da!" she sang, lifting up what appeared to be a man's shaving kit. It was rougher than usual, but that was to be expected with mercenaries. The shaving kit of such a person couldn't be the buttery soft leather kind that his valet packed for him whenever Goran traveled. This one was made of canvas and had several pockets with that Velcro stuff holding it closed. Goran snorted at that.

"What?" Calista asked, startled by his disgusted sound. "What's wrong with this stuff?"

He shook his head. "No, I'm glad that we have something that will allow us to clean up a bit before we enter civilization once again." He focused on down-shifting to get over a particularly rough area of the road. "It's just the Velcro closures."

"What's wrong with that?"

He smiled slightly. "It's not the kind of bag one should take into a combat situation."

She relaxed back against the canvas passenger seat. "Why would anyone bring toiletries into combat?"

"You'd be surprised at the items some people bring into combat. Everyone has their little luxuries. For me, it's shaving supplies. I hate the feel of scruff on my face."

She turned her head, a slight smile to her soft lips that was shockingly sexy. "I kind of like the scruff," she commented.

That surprised him and he glanced at her, only briefly because he really did need to pay attention to the road. "You do?" For a moment, he considered leaving the scruff on his face, which actually shocked him. He'd never changed his mind just to please a woman before. The women in his life changed to please him. And yet, the idea of doing something to make Calista happy was...well, it made him feel good.

"Yeah, but do what makes you comfortable."

"I usually shave twice a day."

She looked at him, startled. "Your beard grows that fast?"

"Yeah."

She laughed, but covered her mouth quickly, turning her face away.

"What?" he growled.

She shook her head, but another snort of laughter tumbled out. "Nothing," she replied, then bent her head to giggle again.

He turned onto the dirt road she'd pointed to on the map.

"Calista, what the hell is so funny?" He slowed the Jeep, downshifted, then accelerated over a rather large log, the thick jungle surrounding them on all sides.

"I just..." she snickered, then recovered but the amusement lingered on her lovely features. "I used to wonder why you seemed to always have such smooth skin!" she laughed again. "I thought the lack of any sort of beard indicated a low testosterone level." She laughed at the low growl, but couldn't contain her amusement any longer. She bent forward, then leaned back, even arching her back as she laughed harder, her shoulders shaking with her mirth.

He turned the corner and came to an abrupt stop, the sound of water coming to them. Her laughter eased and she looked up and...her amusement morphed into an expression of pure pleasure. "Oh my!" she gasped. "What a lovely spot!"

Goran was still looking at her and had to agree, but when she looked over at him, then back out through the windshield, he turned his gaze forward, astonished when he noticed the picturesque scene in front of him. It was straight out of a romantic movie, he thought, his body tightening all over again as he pictured Calista, naked, as the sparkling water tumbled over her bare skin. He could also picture her swimming naked through the clear water in the pool of water created by the waterfall. There were big rocks in several places along the shoreline, but the rest of the shore was made up of tree roots and low hanging branches, making the area look secluded and incredibly exotic. Yeah, he could definitely picture a romantic scene happening here. Or a porn flick!

Banishing that thought from his mind, he put the Jeep in park and shut off the engine. The silence was broken now only by the rushing waterfall while the tension between himself and Calista seemed to increase as they both stared straight ahead.

Calista felt as if her body was on high alert. She could feel the tension thickening in the already teeming air between them. Which was crazy since she suspected that he was just as surprised as she was by their sudden attraction.

And yet, the idea of him seeing her bathe in that water was…well, it was a pretty romantic spot! The area looked as if there was a constant battle between the water and the jungle, both trying to take over the limited space.

"Do you think there are piranha in the water?" she asked, trying to sound teasing, desperate to ease the tension that seemed to be increasing by the moment.

He laughed. "Piranha only live in South America, love. We are pretty safe here," he told her, his voice thicker. Huskier.

She blinked, nodding slowly. "You don't think they might have found their way up here to Costa Rica?"

He shrugged. "There are biting fish off of the coasts. Especially on the Pacific side. But those would be salt water fish."

She turned to look at him and the air seemed to pulse with awareness. "How do you know?"

He shrugged and her eyes dropped to those impressively broad shoulders. "I'm not an ichthyologist, so I can't be positive."

Calista smiled, turned on by his vocabulary. Not many people knew that a scientist who studies fish is called an ichthyologist. "You're a very attractive man," she replied.

"You sound surprised." He had one hand resting on the steering wheel while he watched her, his upper body twisted slightly to observe her reactions.

"I guess…I kind of am," she replied, shyly because she wasn't sure if she was insulting him now. "I mean, I'd thought you were handsome when I'd first met you. And...well, after that first kiss."

A dark eyebrow lifted. "But after that, the attraction waned." It was a statement, not a question.

She nodded ever so slightly. "You felt it too, didn't you?"

He stared at her and Calista held her breath, wondering if he'd be honest with her. Finally, he nodded his head. "Yes. I'd become...concerned...about the potential success of a relationship between us."

Calista breathed out a sigh of relief. "Thank you for that."

He chuckled. "For telling you that I was concerned?"

"For being honest with me. I could feel your distance whenever I was with you. It was as if you didn't want to touch me." She saw the surprise in his eyes and she straightened. "That's okay though!" she stared out through the windshield, rushing her words so that she could explain. "I felt the same way. It was...well, we'd just...I think..."

She stopped because he'd used his free hand to wrap around her neck, pulling her close for a long, soul-drugging kiss. Calista couldn't breathe, she couldn't even move! His mouth was...magical! Or maybe it was just the moment, the romantic atmosphere or something more elusive. But she leaned into him, kissing him back with all of the crazy need that seemed to swell up in her body at the merest touch from this man.

When he lifted his mouth to stare down at her, Calista sighed. Her lips felt swollen and she was almost angry that he'd stopped kissing her.

"Are you worried about my testosterone levels now?"

The question was so completely outside of anything she was expecting that Calista couldn't stop the laughter. It burst out of her and she leaned back, grateful for the release of that mind-clogging tension. "No. I have no fear for your testosterone levels, Goran."

"Good." He grumbled about something, then turned to push open the door. "Let's get cleaned up and formulate a plan."

Calista watched, fascinated as Goran stepped out of the Jeep and immediately started to strip off his sweat-soaked clothing. He moved to the back of the Jeep and rummaged through the other supplies. There were some other clothes, but the other cargo pants he pulled out of a bag were too short for his much longer legs so he tossed them to her. "These will probably fit you better." He found a tan tee-shirt and tossed it over one shoulder, then tossed her another.

"The tee-shirt will fit you?"

He grunted. "The material will stretch enough until we can get new clothes."

She leaned one side of her body against the grubby Jeep, unconcerned about the filth now. She was probably dirtier than the Jeep and they

49

were about to clean up, so what did a bit more grime matter?

"I've been thinking about that. If we call my brother and he sends someone to come get us…"

He filled in when she paused, "Then everyone will know that we're alive and will become a larger target."

"Exactly." She straightened when he waved her towards the water. "I mentioned this suggestion before, but it bears another mention. What if we continue to hide out here while Astir does some careful digging? He'll use his resources to investigate who wanted one of us out of the way. It's more likely you," she said with an impish grin. "You're such an annoying man!"

He growled, then swatted her butt. "You'll get used to my annoying ways," he ordered.

Calista jumped slightly at the unexpected sting from his hand, but the swat actually turned her on more. Or maybe it was the tough-guy manner he was displaying now. The gentleman was definitely still around, but that side of Goran's personality wasn't smothering the other parts. He was looser now. His shoulders weren't as tight, his whole body more relaxed. It was an astonishing realization. They were out in the middle of a jungle with none of their normal luxuries and…and he was relaxed!

With a start, she realized that she was more relaxed as well. In fact, she hadn't felt this relaxed and alive in…a long, long time!

"Well I don't want to get used to your annoying ways?" she teased right back.

He grunted again and she was starting to kind of like those grunts. "You will."

She laughed again, but then stopped when he stood by the edge of the small lake and continued stripping off his clothes. The sweat stained dress shirt was whipped off of his shoulders and bundled up to be tossed onto a big rock. He then stripped off his slacks but he was a bit more careful with that piece of clothing, protectively laying the pants on the rock, probably because he'll need to wear them again soon.

"Aren't you going to get undressed?" he asked, glancing over at her.

A moment later, his fingers looped into the waistband of his boxers and…without any hesitation, he pushed them to the ground.

Calista couldn't stop the startled squeak as she spun around, giving him her back. "I'll…uh…just…uh…wait until you're done. Then I'll take a turn."

She could picture him shrugging those now-delicious shoulders as he said, "Suit yourself." A moment later, she heard a splash and her very imaginative mind pictured his strong, lithe body diving into the water, completely unconcerned with any potential dangers.

"Come on in Calista," he called out to her. "The water is cold and refreshing. I promise not to peek as you strip off your clothes."

Calista peered over her shoulder at him and saw that he was already swimming towards the middle of the water. The tempting promise of cool water was too much for her. Plus, he wasn't paying any attention to her, she thought. So why wait? Why not get into that glorious water and find a bit of relief from this sweltering heat? She'd been hot and sweaty for so long, she wasn't even sure what it would feel like to be clean again!

"Fine!" she grumbled, but turned her back and started to pull off her own clothes. The black cargo pants were carefully laid out on the rock for easy access to post-swimming dressing. She brought her panties and bra into the water with her, needing to clean them. She was pretty desperate for clean underwear and thought that she could lay them out on one of the rocks to dry afterwards. The material was thin enough so it should dry relatively quickly.

Calista wasn't brave enough to dive into the water, but she waded carefully along the water's bank, her feet feeling out the rocks and tree branches visible underneath the glassy water. Thankfully, everything under the water was pretty smooth and nothing poked her skin too hard. But when she was knee deep in the water, she didn't want to feel anything more. She was a bit freaked out at the possibility of something slithering up between the branches to nibble on her toes, so she pushed off, submerging herself in the cool water. Instantly, she felt better! Ducking her head under, she got her hair wet, her fingers clutching at her underwear and the soap she'd found in the shaving kit.

"Oh this feels..." Something brushed against her leg and she screamed, shifting away and trying to figure out what it was. A moment later, a strong arm wrapped around her waist, pulling her against a hard chest. "Relax," Goran's voice rasped into her ear. "I won't hurt you."

Calista stiffened, feeling every naked part of him against her back. "You said you wouldn't look!"

He laughed and she felt his thumb slide against her lower ribs as he pulled her backwards, swimming on his back. "I promised not to look while you undressed," he corrected. She felt him kiss her neck and nip lightly against her earlobe. "I never promised not to look, or touch, once you were in the water."

Calista was shocked and...fascinated! "Um...we have a problem, Goran," she whispered, unable to make her voice any stronger.

"What's that?" he asked, his arm "slipping" higher so that his forearm was right under her breasts. Still not touching, but Calista suddenly realized that she wanted him to touch her! In fact, her breasts seemed to swell with the need for his big, strong, capable hands to touch her breasts! Her nipples ached with the hope that he'd touch her!

Problem. What was the problem? Was there a problem? At this moment, all her mind could think of as a problem is that his hands weren't touching her breasts!

His teeth scraped against her neck, sending delicious shivers through her body. "Um...!"

"I don't see any problem, love," he replied, his hands moving higher.

Suddenly, Calista jerked, shocked by the touch of his hands on her breasts. They were soft, but firm as his fingers cupped their weight, the water swishing around them. They were kept afloat only because Goran's legs were pushing them through the water. If he hadn't been doing that, they'd probably both drown because Calista was incapable of helping to keep them out of that predicament.

"Soap," she groaned, her eyes closing as his thumb and forefinger pinched one nipple, then soothed it by rubbing over the now-turgid peak.

"What about the soap?" he asked, his mouth moving over her neck, increasing the pressure with his fingers.

"Dropped it," she moaned, her mind completely absorbed with his fingers.

"That's going to be an issue." His hands moved lower, brushing over her stomach before coming back to her other breast. She moaned and felt a rising tension in her body. Arching into his hand, she pressed her own hand over his, silently begging him to touch her, showing him what she needed. And boy did she need!

When his hand moved lower, those deft fingers were like magic triggers on her body. Or perhaps she'd been waiting for this moment ever since she'd seen Goran take down the guard. She'd needed him to show her his masculine side for months! She'd given up hope that her fiancé would have a strong side to his personality, something she'd seen in her own brother too many times. Calista couldn't help the fact that she needed a mate who was strong and powerful. It was all she knew in a man. She'd had two role models, her father and brother. They were both alpha males and...!

Oh dear heaven, Goran's fingers moved into that spot between her legs. Calista couldn't stop her legs from shifting, her hand plastered over his. For a brief moment, she wanted to pull his hand away. But then his finger touched that spot, that private space that she'd touched so many times, but this...this was one thousand times better! More exciting, more dangerous, more tantalizing!

One finger slid into her heat and she gasped, shocked by the slight invasion. But while his finger slid in and out, his thumb rubbed that spot. She shifted, her hand closing over his thumb. Calista was mindless now, desperate for that release, needing it more than her next breath! With a skill she couldn't have anticipated, Goran teased and tortured that nub, his fingers moving against her with the perfect pressure. If he moved too fast, she slowed him down. When she needed him to shift that magical thumb faster, she showed him. When the climax burst over her, she arched her back, her body shivering as the pleasure rode through her like a wave of beautiful wonder!

And throughout the whole experience, Goran held her steady, cradled against his chest, his fingers withdrawing while his thumb slowed and, eventually, stopped. His touch was soothing now, helping to bring out the last breath of pleasure as she shifted, turning herself around to look at him.

Instantly, a blush crept up over her cheeks. She pushed under the water for a moment, hoping it would cool down the blush. Pushing the water out of her eyes, she looked back at him. He was staring at her, his eyes hot and heavy as undiminished lust still rode his body.

"Thank you!" she whispered, her hands sliding up over his chest. She realized that he was no longer swimming, but his hand was holding onto a thick branch that had grown into an arch that dipped down into the water.

"You're welcome," he replied, his voice thick and husky. Sexy!

She touched his chest, her fingers inching along every ridge, feeling the muscle twitch as she explored. No other words were spoken as they stared at each other. His hand on the branch continued to hold them in place while she let her fingers move over his hard body, lower and lower until she found his erection. He uttered a hiss as her fingers closed over that member and his free hand came down, doing the same thing that her hand had done. Her gentle fingers were only lightly wrapped around his shaft. But he guided her fingers, tightening her grip as he showed her how to stroke him, where he liked to be touched. Very quickly, she figured it out and he released her hand, but his eyes never left her gaze. He stared at her, silently commanding her to keep going. Her hand tightened and his jaw clenched. She heard him groan, but he kept his eyes on her, their dark depths powerfully heated and intense as she stroked him, her fingers fumbling slightly since she wasn't exactly sure what she was doing, but she figured he'd stop her if she did something wrong.

His hand moved the water around them, his body tightening with every stroke of her fingers. Up and down, she teased him, letting her finger smooth over the tip, then searching blindly against the underside of that ridge. It was all so fascinating, but too soon, he reached under the water and controlled her hand, moving her fingers harder, faster. She moved closer, her body thrumming with anticipation. But she wasn't exactly sure what she might be anticipating.

And then it happened. His body tightened, his eyes closed and his hand continued to guide hers, but she knew he was climaxing under the water. She wanted to move closer to him, to wrap her whole body around his. The moment was powerfully intimate and yet, she was touching him only on his erection.

A moment later, it was over and he groaned. His eyes opened, but they were more relaxed now. In fact, his whole body was less tense and his arm whipped around her waist, pulling her against him. Yes, she thought, this is what she wanted, what she needed right at this moment. With unhesitating swiftness, she lifted her mouth up for his kiss, showing him how delighted she was by their actions. He kissed her softly, slowly and oh so thoroughly! It wasn't a kiss of a desire. It was a kiss of gratitude. They'd shared something here this morning and Calista was more fascinated by the man than she'd ever thought possible.

"Thank you," he whispered roughly against her lips.

Calista smiled, feeling daring and courageous. "Thank *you*," she replied back with just as much emphasis. And then he was kissing her again, his mouth slanting over hers, the water swishing around them. His body was hot and secure while the water was cold and silky. The contrast was...shockingly erotic. Even though her body had so recently been satisfied, Calista knew a rising sense of need, so she pulled back, embarrassed and confused.

"Are you okay?" he asked, releasing his arm from around her waist, but holding her hands to keep her afloat.

"Yes," she replied, swimming backwards towards the center of the water. "I should...I need to find the soap." It was a lame excuse but she couldn't think of anything else to say. Other than to plead with him to come back onto the shore so they could do that all over again.

But that didn't make sense! She couldn't want him again! Not so soon. Could she?

"Why don't you let me search for the soap," he called out, pushing off of the rock next to him, then coming towards her in strong, powerful strokes of his arms. When he reached her, he stopped and lifted his head, looking around. "Is this where I made you drop the soap?"

She smiled slightly, unable to look him in the eye. "Yes. I think so, but I can't be completely sure."

"I'll go down and see if I can find it. I'm pretty sure that a bar of soap will feel different than the other things that are at the bottom of this water."

A second later, he disappeared under the water. He was submerged for so long, Calista started to become concerned. Could he really hold his breath for that long? What if he'd gotten caught on something down there? She knew that the trees and branches, not to mention other debris from storms over the years were down there, just rotting away in the jungle waters. Were there alligators here? Or crocodiles? Or were crocodiles only in Australia? Oh, why hadn't she paid more attention during her geography lessons?!

She was just about to dive under the water when he popped up right next to her. "Found it," he said while shaking his head to displace the water from his face. A moment later, he held the soap up triumphantly, a handsome grin on his features. "I couldn't find your panties though."

Calista gave him a mock glare. "You don't seem very upset about that," she grumbled, taking the soap from his hand. For several moments, she rubbed the soap along her skin, rubbing the dirt and grime away and instantly feeling better. She handed the soap to him as she dove under the water to rinse the soap off.

When she was all cleaned up, Calista headed back towards the area where she'd waded into the water, but didn't walk out. For some reason, despite the intimacies they'd just shared, Calista simply couldn't step out from the protection the water provided. She simply couldn't walk along that shoreline naked! Not with Goran watching her. And yes, she was fairly certain that he wouldn't turn away from her this time. He wouldn't give her that small bit of privacy.

"I'll admit that the thought of you walking through the jungle, totally commando in the best sense of the word, is pretty hot."

Calista peered at him over her shoulder, a smile lingering on her features. "You're not being very gentlemanly, are you?"

"You don't want a gentleman," he replied, his voice dangerously close once more. He then snatched the soap out of her hands and started lathering himself. She wanted to turn and watch him, but knew that her body was still too...stimulated. Oh, what a crass word, she thought. And yet, there was no other way to describe how her body was vibrating with eagerness to run her hands over his chest, to feel his body against hers. The soap would make everything much more slick, more enticing.

"I'm ready to get out," she announced, hoping he'd offer to turn around and let her get dressed without him staring at her.

"Go for it," he replied. "I'm right behind you."

Exactly what she was afraid of. With a sigh, she turned and pushed off towards the center again. "Maybe I'll just go for a swim. I don't want to be sweaty and dirty again and this water is pretty nice."

"Coward," he replied with a chuckle. Obviously, he saw right through her ruse.

Calista swam a bit away, but then turned, treading water as she watched him walk out of the water. His butt was a work of art, she thought, watching the flexing muscles. His back was just as nice and his thighs more powerful than she could have imagined. Why had she thought him lacking in power? Why had she been disdainful of him for so long? How could she not have seen all of those muscles underneath his tailored suits? It seemed impossible now, as he dried himself off with his dress shirt before pulling on his slacks, leaving the boxers off. Goodness, now she'd know that he had nothing on underneath! Yeah, that was hot!

"We need to find a place to get a phone, Calista," he called out, startling her as he turned around, pulling the tee shirt over his head. The material stretched, desperately trying to cover all of those muscles on his shoulders and arms. His waist was lean and taut, the material hanging loosely there. But goodness, those shoulders were...!

"Calista?" he called out, fisting his hands on his hips. "We need to go."

"I'm coming," she called back, swimming towards that spot. He watched her and, when she reached the place where she would have to start walking out, she stopped. "I can't do it, Goran."

"Can't do what?" he asked, but the smirk on his handsome features warned her that he knew exactly what she was talking about.

"I can't come out while you watch me."

He laughed, shaking his head, but thankfully, he turned around.

Quickly, she stepped out of the water, grabbing his shirt and using it to dry off as best she could. Unfortunately, she'd lost both her panties and her bra under the water. Why had she thought it was so essential to wash her underwear? Obviously, she'd been wrong. But she pulled the clean tee shirt over her head, cringing at the way the material clung to her damp skin. The cargo pants were easier to pull on because they were loose around her waist, but the now damp tee shirt made it obvious that she wasn't wearing a bra. "I'm covered," she told him, bending down to brush her feet off before slipping them into the boots.

"Nice," he commented, then turned toward the Jeep. "Now we just need to figure out a good place to steal a phone and make a call to your brother." He pulled the map out to examine the details. "Here," he said, pointing to a place near the coastline. "There's a resort here. I can sneak onto the grounds and find a phone. Maybe I won't have to steal a cell phone if I can break into one of the offices and make the call from there." He folded the map, his eyes scanning the other equipment in the Jeep. "That would actually be better. It's harder to trace a call from a specific person from a landline."

Calista pulled one of the cans of food out of the pillow cases. "How about some..." she looked at the label. "This doesn't look like any ravioli I've ever eaten," she said with a shrug. "But I'm pretty sure it's edible." She tossed him a can with the same red label, then dug the can opener out of the bag. They didn't have forks, but Calista discovered that the faux Italian meal was simple enough to eat with her fingers. They turned orange from the overly sweet sauce, but that was okay. The food satisfied the hunger and she reached for a bottle of water. "That was better than I would have thought," she commented as she tossed him a water bottle as well.

"I agree, but I wouldn't mind a thick, juicy steak."

She ignored the pang of longing his words created and searched through the rest of the supplies. "I don't see anything else that might help in our stealth plan, so let's just get this over with."

"I need a status update!" Neville demanded, his voice tinny over the burner phone.

Ned rolled his eyes and turned away from the site of the enormous trucks and drills and other mining equipment that was currently shuttling down the hill. Somehow he was supposed to hide this stuff? He shook his head and mentally laughed.

"Everything is going according to plan," he assured the man. Ned glanced at his watch and wondered why he hadn't received an update from his team in Costa Rico. They were five minutes late.

Looking up again, he pointed towards the east end of the staging area, silently ordering one of the drivers to park his massive truck in that area. "Look Neville, I have twenty trucks and five drills that I need to get covered up before the next satellite pass. That's going to happen in exactly five hours and twenty-six minutes. Is there anything else you need to know?"

Ned could almost hear the old man's yellowed teeth gnashing together. Ned just wasn't the kind of man who could come up with a subservient tone while talking, especially when speaking to this old bastard.

"No. Your assurance that everything is on schedule is all I need to hear." The call ended after that and Ned shook his head while stuffing the phone back into his pocket. But he made a mental note to call his team down in Costa Rica in ten minutes if he didn't hear something from them. There wasn't any chance that the two prisoners had escaped. He'd built a freaking tree house to ensure that they couldn't! It was like a jungle Alcatraz! Even if el Istara and his princess somehow came out of their drug induced sedation, they'd then have to break free from the plastic zip ties, take down his highly trained guards and somehow get down from the shelter that he'd had his men build into the tree's canopy. The ladder was removed by the guards on the ground. Without the ladder, his prisoners would break their legs, as well as several other bones, if either of them tried to jump in order to escape.

"Sir!" one of the mining experts called out, running over to Ned and looking as if he'd just come through a sand storm. The guy had a thick layer of dust covering him, which was expected since driving these massive trucks kicked up a lot of dust. Which was why Ned stood here on this dirt mound, well out of the way from the dust that was finally settling now that the trucks were parked.

"What is it?" Ned demanded, crossing his arms over his chest as a way to deter idle chit chat. For the next several hours, he handled issues in order to get all of the equipment hidden so that they could settle down for an hour or two before getting back to work. Everything had to be silent and non-moving before the satellites passed overhead or this operation was finished!

Chapter 5

Calista paced back and forth across the dirt, kicking at small rocks as her mind went through a series of horrible possibilities. Goran had snuck over the concrete wall surrounding the most luxurious resort they'd come across and she was waiting here until he came back. Had he found a phone yet? What was taking him so long? Or had he been arrested? And if he was arrested, could he convince the guards of who he was? If he had to reveal his identity, was he now in danger once again?

The questions and possibilities flew through her mind, tumbling over each other as she paced back and forth. She didn't have a watch, so Calista had no idea how long she'd been standing there, hidden at the edge of the jungle. One thing she knew for sure though, she didn't like being out in the creepy jungle after dark by herself! This was down-right scary! Although, if Goran were here with her, she wouldn't be nearly as concerned. There was just an aura of confidence surrounding him. A sensation that he knew how to handle every situation that might arise.

Calista had just decided to jump back into the Jeep and head out to find him when a dark shadow emerged from the darkness. Calista almost screamed in fright, but Goran's features emerged from the moonlight and she was able to stifle her startled scream.

"You okay?" he asked, pulling her into his arms.

Instantly, Calista was reassured and she pressed her body against his strong frame, nestling her face against the warmth of his neck.

"Yes," she replied, but there was a note in her voice that contradicted her claim.

"Sorry it took so long," he replied, kissing the top of her head. "We're further away from the resort buildings than I thought. Then it took me several minutes to explain everything to your brother and assure him that you were safe. He wanted to send out the military immediately, but I explained our plan and got him to agree." Goran pulled back, brushing her hair out of her face. "He's working some back-channel sources and someone will arrange for us to have a private cabana here at the resort, but far enough away from the other resort guests so we're not recognized."

"Oh, that's such a relief!" she sighed, snuggling in a bit closer. "Will there be coffee?" she asked, smothering a yawn.

Goran laughed, rubbing a hand up and down her back. "Yes. I'll make sure that there is fresh coffee tomorrow morning."

"You're a good man," she replied. "And did you tell Astir where to find the tied-up guards?"

Goran chuckled. "Yes, Pollyanna. I've ensured that they will be picked up and questioned."

"Thank you, G.I. Joe."

He hugged her closer for another moment, then released her. "We should be able to head into the resort now. Enough time has passed for the calls to be made, but we'll still need to be careful in order to maintain our anonymity."

"A bed," she sighed with happy longing. "A real bed!"

He took her hand and led her over to the Jeep. "It's not as if you've had to sleep without a bed yet," he teased her.

"I guess being drugged and unconscious doesn't count? But yeah, it feels as if we've been gone for weeks!"

Goran agreed with her there, he thought as he walked around to the driver's side and started the engine. The noise was loud in the night air, but he wanted to get Calista to a safe place, then hide this vehicle so that it couldn't be found again. He wanted her safe, and he wanted good food. She'd been such a trooper over the past twenty-four hours, maybe longer. Now he was going to pamper her until she begged for mercy!

Calista sighed as she stepped into the lovely cabana. The tiled floor was clean and cool as she walked across it, having slipped off the clunky, filthy boots outside the door. "Oh, this is heavenly!" she gasped, looking around at the spacious area. "I'm not sure what we're going to do with a kitchen, but I like the idea of the bed looking out at the ocean."

She stopped, staring at the bed. One bed! She didn't dare turn around. No way could she look at Goran's reaction. After that erotic interlude in the water earlier today, she wasn't sure what he expected of her.

"Why don't you take a shower? There should be a robe in the bath-room, so you don't have to put those clothes back on."

That sounded wonderful and she moved into the bathroom, not bothering to point out the single bed right now. At the moment, her priority was to get clean. Even after the "bath" in the waterfall earlier today, she still felt hot and sticky. They'd driven for four hours in the hot sun to reach this resort and, with no air conditioning in the military style Jeep, the only cooling feature was the open windows. It was bet-ter than nothing, and she was definitely grateful that they hadn't had to walk out of that horrible jungle. It had been a stroke of luck for the other guards to arrive just at the same moment she and Goran had been escaping.

Stepping into the bathroom, she stripped off her sweaty clothes and went straight under the shower. There were bottles of complimentary shampoo and conditioner, scented soaps and even lotion! Oh yes, she thought and scrubbed her body clean. There was indeed a white, fluffy robe folded on the countertop. Two, actually. That was good because Calista wasn't sure she could handle watching Goran walk around the cabana completely naked. She'd barely recovered from watching him earlier this afternoon.

When she stepped out of the bathroom, she found Goran on the phone. Where had he gotten a cell phone? She was too tired to think about it anymore. She tightened the belt on her robe and padded over to the bed. Calista promised herself that she'd lay down for just a mo-ment. Just long enough to recover a bit. It had been a long day. They'd been up for...maybe twenty hours now? So yeah, she'd take a quick, ten minute nap, then talk to Goran about the next steps.

Goran stepped into the bedroom and came to an abrupt halt. He'd been about to tell Calista about his latest phone call with her brother as well as his own intelligence unit but instead, he found her sound asleep, wrapped up in the thick, terrycloth robe but with one leg escaping from the edges. She looked...beautiful. Peaceful.

For a long time, he simply stood there, staring down at her, looking at each of her features. Her face was softer, the tension leaving her face and making her appear much more approachable. Of course, he wouldn't wake her up. The past...however long they'd been gone...had been extremely stressful. For both of them, and yet, he felt wired, need-ing to do something to fix this situation.

Unfortunately, the best course of action was for him to sit back and allow Astir and his security team to work the investigation. He wasn't used to letting someone else take charge. But in this instance, Goran knew that it was best. Plus, he trusted Astir to find out why the hell he and Calista had been kidnapped. Both men had their suspicions, but they needed proof.

So instead of heading out into the darkness, Goran turned and stepped into the bathroom. He showered, thoughts turning around in his mind as he tried to put the pieces of the puzzle together. He'd started to become concerned about a mining company that had asked for permission to mine for some minerals in the eastern portion of his country. That alone didn't seem like an odd request though. Mining companies were a part of every country's economy. The companies provided good jobs and a substantial tax revenue. Mining companies weren't the evil entities that most people thought. But there was something about the way this company had approached his officials that bothered Goran. Although, what that issue was, he couldn't quite put his finger on it. Not yet, anyway.

Could this new mining company be related to the secretive company that had wreaked havoc in Silar recently? That company had drilled too close to a small village and too close to the surface without adequate supports to reinforce the dig. The whole town had collapsed into what aid workers had originally thought was an unknown sink hole. But when Astir's people had investigated, they'd discovered that it was an illegal mine trying to pull efiasia out of the earth. Efiasia was a mineral that unethical computer manufacturers used to build the microchips that powered their laptops. Efiasia worked as an efficient conductor of energy, but it broke down much faster than other minerals, making the computer unusable after about two years.

Goran sipped a glass of excellent scotch as he looked out into the darkness. He could hear the waves crashing against the shoreline, but his mind was focused on the current problem. What was it about this newest mining request that bothered him so much? After the debacle in Silar, Goran had put all new mining requests on hold, pending more thorough investigations.

So what was bothering him? And could that one mining request have something to do with his current kidnapping? The two seemed completely unrelated. Why would someone who wanted to mine in Skyla do something so drastic as kidnap him? It would make more sense to kidnap the head of his Department of Minerals and Mining.

And yet, something was warning him that the two issues were related. Yesterday, when they were trying to get out of the "tree-house", he hadn't thought anything about the latest mining request. But now that he was relatively safe and Calista was sleeping in a soft bed where he could see her, could know that she was safe and secure...his mind now had the capacity to think through the details. Yes, something about that request bothered him

He just needed to discover the connection, if there was one. He could just be imagining a connection. Hell, he wasn't even imagining anything in particular. It was just a gut feeling that the two were connected.

He'd learned to pay attention to his gut. It was never wrong.

Tossing down the rest of his scotch, he turned and looked at Calista, something shifting inside of his chest. She was...so different than what he'd assumed. She was so much...more!

Turning with a sigh, he put his glass down on the dresser and moved into the bathroom. He was definitely too tired to figure this out right now. He needed sleep and to eat some food before he could think properly. And perhaps spend several days alone with Calista, where neither of them got out of bed as they explored each other without all of the restrictions of real life.

He finished drying off and wrapped the towel around his waist. Rubbing a hand over his face, he reached for the razor provided by the resort but...then he set it down. Goran remembered Calista's comments about his features. What the hell had she said? That he'd looked effeminate? No, her words hadn't gone that far. She'd merely said that she'd thought he lacked testosterone.

Hell, it was the opposite, he thought as he walked out of the bathroom. He took one of the throw blankets and laid it over her legs. The blanket covered her all the way up to her waist. Adjusting the air conditioning down a couple more degrees, he then went around and turned off all of the lights. Tossing the towel over onto one of the chairs, he moved to the opposite side of the bed and slipped under the covers. Pulling Calista closer. Even after what they'd done at the waterfall earlier today, Goran knew that Calista wasn't ready for a truly intimate relationship quite yet. He'd let her sleep on top of the covers while he slept under the sheet. If she woke up in the middle of the night, the material separating them would reassure her that he had no intention of taking advantage of her while she slept.

That wasn't entirely true, he thought as he adjusted her body so that she was draped more completely over his, smiling into the darkness when she snuggled even closer. Hell, his entire body, mind and soul were ready with numerous evil intentions. Okay, maybe not evil as much as naughty. Salacious. Lascivious intentions!

Sighing, he pushed all of those thoughts from his mind. Or, he tried to at least. Where Calista was concerned, he was starting to realize that pushing those thoughts from his mind was an exercise in futility. They came back too quickly. Too easily.

How his world had changed in the past two days! He'd gone from needing to extricate himself from his engagement to this woman, to needing to keep her close.

Ned ended the call and turned, furious at the lack of news. "How the hell did they escape?" he muttered, then walked over to his laptop. He flipped through several news websites. "Nothing!" There was no news about an abduction, but also no news about the leader of Skyla coming back.

He flipped over to a different page, one that contained the sheik's personal schedule. Getting this information had required massive bribes to several individuals, but the details had been well worth the cost. Unfortunately, the Sheik of Skyla didn't have any public appearances scheduled for today.

Since he hadn't heard from his guards in Costa Rica, and the sheik hadn't arrived back home…? That wasn't good, Ned thought. He'd counted on his team of highly trained men to keep the sheik and his fiancée tied up and sedated. But after twenty-four hours without any updates, Ned had to conclude that something had gone wrong.

He made another call. "I need you to go out to the coordinates I'm going to send to you," he told the person who answered the call. "Once you get there, call me back and tell me what you find."

Ned stuffed his phone back into his pocket, then headed out of his tent. He had work to do. That crap mineral that the old man wanted so badly wasn't going to miraculously sift itself out of the dirt and sand and pop into the trucks.

Time to start digging!

Chapter 6

Calista sighed, feeling sore and warm and strangely content. She hadn't felt this relaxed in...ever!

Snuggling into the warmth, she pressed her nose against something that smelled incredibly good. But what was that heavy object laying over her waist? Calista didn't want to wake up enough to find out, so she pressed herself closer to that warmth again. There was something odd about the morning, but she couldn't quite put her finger on the problem. But was it really a problem when everything felt this good?

The soft, butterfly kisses along her neck should have been a warning. But...well, they felt really good! She shifted her head, wanting more of those kisses. Strong fingers slid against her stomach, sending darts of need along her nerve endings. Okay, that wasn't exactly "comfortable", but it felt wonderful!

Rolling over, she forced her eyes to open, needing to investigate whatever was happening.

As soon as her lashes lifted, her fingers dove into Goran's soft hair.

"You're awake, right?" he asked, barely lifting his mouth from the soft skin of her throat. "I thought you'd never wake up!"

She laughed, but was there anything funny about this? Calista was suddenly so turned on, her laughter turned into a moan of pleasure.

"Do you want me to stop?" he asked, pulling his hand away. Calista grabbed his hand, placing it back onto her bare stomach. "Don't stop!" she whispered, turning so that she could press herself against him.

Goran wasn't about to stop, so he shifted their position, moving so that he was on top of her and pressing his leg between her thighs, spreading her legs.

"Goran!" she gasped, arching up, pressing her core against his hard thigh. He pressed his leg against her, understanding what she was

65

doing. He wanted to see and feel her explode this time. Yesterday, the water had hindered his view of her body as she'd climaxed. He wasn't going to lose that pleasure this time. He pushed the sheets out of the way and spread the already loose robe away from her lovely body.

Her breasts were beautiful! Tipped with dark tan nipples, he lowered his head, tasting one tip, then the other. She gasped and pressed her breasts deeper into his mouth, arching her back and shifting her hips against his thigh.

"Tell me what you like," he whispered into her ear, then moved lower, his hot mouth sucking on the peak of her breast.

"That!" she gasped. "I like that!"

His other hand covered her breast, soothing and pinching, teasing the nipple while his mouth covered the tip, his tongue flicking against the puckered peak, making her groan as she tried to handle both sensations.

"This is...crazy!" she moaned.

"This is hot," Goran countered, shifting against her core, creating sparks of intense pleasure and frustration down below.

Lifting her hips, Calista wrapped her legs around his hips, pressing herself against him. "I need...something!"

Goran pressed against her, his body shifting but it wasn't enough. Calista needed something...she wasn't sure how to handle whatever was happening to her. It was all too new and too...shocking!

"Relax," Goran soothed, moving lower.

"I don't...this isn't going to work!" she told him, but her inner thighs rubbed against his hips, her body trying to find some sort of release.

He laughed softly, then lowered his head to nibble along her shoulder. "I promise, I'm very good at making this work."

She sighed, tilting her head back. "You're....ahhh!" she gasped when he bit her. Then he moved his mouth lower and she couldn't seem to stop him. Calista wasn't even sure if she wanted to stop him! Her body remembered yesterday. The waterfall. His hands...dear heaven he knew how to use his hands! Those fingers should be illegal!

"What am I, love?" he asked softly, but he didn't stop to hear her answer. He continued moving along her shoulders, nipping and tasting, sending bolts of desire through her body so fast, she couldn't seem to think properly.

"You're doing things that...!" she couldn't finish that sentence because he'd just moved down to her stomach, teasing the soft skin, nibbling on her hip bone.

"Tell me what I'm doing to you," he urged, his hands sliding down over the skin of her thighs. "You have the softest skin I've ever felt."

Calista wanted to order him to stop comparing her to the other women he'd been with. She didn't want to know if their skin had been rough or soft or felt like satin. She just wanted him to...yeah! That! She wanted him to do that!

His mouth moved even lower, his shoulders pushing her legs wider. "You're not telling me what I'm doing to you, *habibi*," he commented, as if they were having a casual conversation over a cup of coffee instead of his mouth moving lower, doing intimate, insanely lovely things to her body! Not to mention, why was he calling her his "love"? She wasn't! And that was...!

"You have to stop!" she gasped, trying to wiggle away from him. But the huge robe she'd fallen asleep in last night, plus his strong hands holding her still, made her efforts useless. Her fingers fumbled, trying to find something to hold onto, but it was just his shoulders, his hair and...and dear heaven what was he doing now?!

"I'm not going to stop," he warned her, his hands moving hers out of the way so that his mouth could move along her pink folds unhindered. "Remember yesterday?" he whispered, then blew on her wetness.

"Yes!" she gasped, arching her hips. Was she confirming that she remembered what they'd done yesterday? Or was she crying out her delight in what he was doing now? She wasn't sure, so she couldn't really answer him now.

"Well, I want to see what you look like when that happens today."

She lifted her head, looking down at him. But he wasn't watching her. His eyes were intent on her body, his mouth moving lower again as if he were intent on finding his own pleasure, simply by giving her pleasure.

"You taste like honey," he commented, then moved closer, his mouth closing over her, his tongue lashing out, diving in and tasting her core, then sliding higher, lower, moving all around that nub. She wanted to scream out, her body straining against his mouth. She was so close, she felt as if even one more touch would send her right over the edge. He must have known how close she was because he pulled back.

"You're...!'

He grinned, lifting his head again. Did he really just lick his lips? Damn him, he was enjoying this!

"Yes?" he inquired. But she couldn't reprimand him for his cruel treatment of her because he slipped one finger into her body, sliding it in and...and...and what the hell was he doing to her? She was out of control, her body shifting against his hand. His mouth closed over that nub once more, sucking and licking, lapping at the overly sensitive bud. She screamed, straining and...this time, he let her tumble over to a climax that was so strong, so powerful, she could only feel. There was no controlling this moment. It was sheer pleasure and her body throbbed with a glorious release.

Her whole body stretched, her mind blanking and all she could feel was his hands touching her, his lips kissing a path back up her body as her climax slowly receded.

When Calista finally opened her eyes once more, it was to find Goran looking down at her with a smug, triumphant look to his eyes. "What were you saying about not being able to do something?" he teased.

She started to groan, but he merely nudged her legs wider, taking her hands in his and lifting them up over her head. She felt his erection against her legs and, impossibly, that was all it took to regain her attention. "You're truly evil," she whispered.

He laughed, but that sound shifted to a kiss as he smothered any other objection with his mouth. Boy, had she thought he knew what to do with his hands? The man was an excellent kisser! His lips moved from demanding to coaxing in seconds, then back to demanding as he shifted against her body, pressing himself closer and closer but not entering her.

Calista groaned, but she didn't want this moment to end. It was just too...beautiful! She'd been with other men before, but nothing compared to this experience. She wanted it to last forever! This time, this moment together...it was just a moment with him but it was all she had. It was all she'd get! So Calista was determined to make the most of it.

Pressing her hands against his shoulders, she pressed him back onto the mattress, her body straddling his. That magnificent erection she'd felt yesterday was there, right between them, straining against her body.

"You're...magnificent," she whispered to him, her eyes moving over his shoulders and chest, covered with just a dusting of hair. Goodness, she loved a man with a powerful chest! "I want to taste you," she warned mere moments before she lowered her head, letting her lips drift against his chest. He tasted clean, but with a hint of salt. And all male! Inhaling, Calista tried to memorize the scent of him, wishing she could bottle his masculine scent and keep it for the future. It was powerfully sexy. There was no cologne to hinder his scent. It was all Goran. And delicious! Heady!

Goran watched as Calista's mouth lowered to his sternum and he almost stopped her. This was insane, he realized. But then her lips touched his skin and he closed his eyes, letting her mouth tease him, her fingers sliding along his arms, then moving onto his stomach. He almost jackknifed up when her fingers wrapped around his shaft. No fooling around with Calista! She was always straight to the point. He might have liked that about her, if he wasn't already in so much pain. Tasting her climax like that, seeing her body writhe against him, had set his whole body on edge. Goran didn't want any teasing. He wanted to flip her back over and let his body slam into hers. He wanted to thrust into her and...what the hell was she doing now?!

He looked at her, his muscles clenching as he watched her mouth move lower. And lower! Was she going to...?

She did! His head fell backwards and he had to close his eyes as her soft, hot mouth closed over his shaft. That tongue...Calista always looked so prim and proper, so uptight and perturbed with her mouth compressed into a thin line. That mouth wasn't compressed now! When he lifted his head again, looking down at her, he acknowledged that she had the sexiest, most beautiful mouth ever! She was a bit clumsy with her efforts, but even that was such a turn on!

She took more of him into her mouth and he just about lost it right then and there. But her hands, which had been floating over his stomach and upper thighs, moved to cup his softness, making his erection even harder! When her tongue, either accidentally or on purpose, flicked against the underside of his shaft, that was all he could take. All common sense was gone as lust overpowered reason. He lifted her up and pushed her back onto the bed. Goran hovered over her for mere moments before he thrust into her.

"You're so damn tight, *habibi!*" he groaned, lifting her leg up so that her inner thigh rested against his hip. Pushing deeper, he blinked, trying to ensure that he wasn't hurting her. She was tight and hot and wet and perfect as she lifted her hips. In the back of his mind, he felt her hands sliding onto his shoulders, then down over his back. But mostly, he felt her body tremble as he thrust into her, pulling back, then thrusting again. And again! She was absolutely perfect and he couldn't slow down! Shaking his head, he tried to concentrate, tried to figure out if she was even close. He heard her scream and moments later, Goran felt her body shudder, her inner muscles clenching around his shaft. That was as long as he could hold off. Moments later, he released that miniscule amount of control and let himself climax as well.

Afterwards, he collapsed against her, then shifted, pulling her onto his chest so that he wasn't smothering her. For a long time, he simply stared up at the ceiling, trying to make sense of the passionate woman who had come apart in his arms, the woman who had made him come apart...and the woman he'd known for the past several months. The coldly detached woman who seemed to be angry with the world.

There were two different women. He didn't understand how she could be so dissimilar at various intervals. Lifting his hand, he tangled his fingers in her mussed hair. In that moment, feeling her soft sighs against his shoulder, Goran made a vow that he was going to understand this woman.

Yes, he also needed to understand what the hell was going on in the world, why they'd been kidnapped and who was behind the kidnaping. And why the hell had they involved Calista. His arms tightened around her, a feeling of intense protectiveness hitting him all of a sudden.

Two mysteries. One, he couldn't do anything about. He couldn't investigate the kidnapping. He had to go against everything he believed in and allow Astir to investigate the kidnapping. Intellectually, Goran trusted Astir to figure this out. But his male pride and his furious anger warned him that he wouldn't be able to relinquish control of the investigation for too long.

However, having Calista here, a distraction and a beautiful mystery as well, he accepted that she was just as intriguing. And it would be significantly more fun to discover Calista's mysteries!

"Are you okay?" he asked now that he could breathe. Decision made, he wanted to know everything about her. In his usual manner, Goran was thorough and efficient. Once he embarked on a plan, he was determined to finish it as quickly as possible.

He felt her stirring against his body, but there was...she was trembling?

Rolling over, he shifted their bodies so that he could see her more clearly. She tried to close her legs, but he wasn't having any of that. No way was he going to allow her to retreat back into that cold persona he'd met before this whole debacle.

"What's wrong?" he demanded, lifting away so that he could look down at her. "Are you hurt? How do you feel?" He started to pull her legs apart, intending to examine her more closely, but Calista gave him a shaky laugh and pulled away, grabbing the sheet to cover her nakedness from him.

"Calista, if you don't tell me what I did to hurt you, I'm going to bundle you up and take you to the hospital!"

She laughed again, but the soft touch of her fingers against his shoulder stopped his fury, easing his concern.

"I'm fine," she told him.

He pulled her closer again, still looking down into her eyes. "You're not fine, Calista. Why are you upset?"

She sighed, but he relaxed slightly when she shifted, still using that damn sheet between their bodies, but she put her head against his chest. It wasn't enough, but it was a start.

"I'm not upset."

He growled, pulling her closer. "Calista, I can feel your body trembling. I hurt you and if you don't tell me how, then..."

"I'm just..." she sighed, her palm coming to rest against his chest. He loved having her touch him. Damn it, he wasn't a cuddly person normally, especially after sex. Once he'd been with a woman and they'd both enjoyed their time together, Goran preferred jumping into a shower and getting back to work. He had very basic needs and he didn't like a woman to distract him once his needs were fulfilled.

Not so with Calista. He wasn't exactly sure what he needed right now, but her hand against his chest was a damn good start. Getting rid of the sheet would also help! He didn't want to feel just small parts of her skin against his. He wanted to feel every inch of her, to know that he could run his hands over her skin and feel her heartbeat against his chest!

"Talk to me, honey," he urged softly, trying to smooth out the rough tone of his voice. He wanted to encourage her to tell him what was wrong, and his voice sounded...gruff. Angry.

"I don't think I can put into words what I'm feeling, Goran," she said.

His frustration with her lack of an explanation eased slightly when her hand slid along his stomach, then came back to rest against his chest once more. It was a good thing that she hadn't left her hand down low because, although he'd had a climax, he was more than ready to explore Calista once again. He craved the sound of her cries when she came to her own satisfaction. It was like an aphrodisiac!

Shifting, he moved over her once more. "Calista..."

She put a hand to his mouth, and he considered biting her fingertips. Not hard, but they tasted good. Instead, he kissed the tips, causing her to smile.

"You climaxed. I know that." He said it, but he also wanted confirmation.

She blushed and turned her head away. "Of course I did. But...?" Just at that moment, her face paled and she looked up at him.

Calista froze as a thought occurred to her. "Goran, by any chance did you...?"

He lifted dark eyebrows at her question, but at least her tone brought his eyes back from her breasts. He couldn't see much because she kept the white sheet covering her body. But she was starting to understand the look in his eyes. He was ready for another round while her body was...well, she was suddenly terrified.

"Did I what?" he asked softly in that deep, gruff voice that she loved.

"Did you...use...protection?" she finally got out, swallowing past the panic that was slowly choking her. They'd gotten into the cabana, but she was pretty sure that the supplies they'd requested hadn't yet been delivered. And just thinking about the food and toiletries that she'd asked for...condoms hadn't been on that list! But had Goran thought to ask for them?

The blank look in his eyes warned her that his mind wasn't going in the same direction as hers.

"Protection? What kind of...?" he stopped, his mind catching up with hers. For a moment, he looked stunned, shocked at the omission. Then his features morphed to grimness and she worried that he wouldn't answer her. But he shook his head. "No. I hadn't thought about it. And even if I had, I don't think I would have remembered." He lowered his head, resting his forehead against her sheet-covered chest. "I'm sorry, Calista. I didn't protect you."

She let her fingers dive into his hair, the softness somehow comforting. "It wasn't your fault," she whispered, her lips numb.

He lifted his head. "What are the odds that something could come of our activities?"

She bit her lower lip, counting back the days. And weeks. With a sigh of relief, she relaxed. "It's okay," she told him. "This is probably the wrong time of the month for me to get pregnant."

He stared at her hard, his eyes searching her features. "Are you sure?"

Calista laughed, her body shifting as much as it could while still wrapped up in a white sheet with a giant man on top of her. "Yeah, I'm pretty sure."

He was serious for another moment, then his features cleared, his eyes lighting up with deviltry. "So...we can try that again?' he asked. "I won't climax inside of you. Even if this is a bad time of the month, I won't put you at risk." He shifted again, his body already hard and ready for another round now that the danger was diminished. "But there are many variations on that previous theme that could be...interesting to explore."

Calista laughed, shaking her head. "I think I'm a bit too sore for another round."

His eyes turned serious. "You said that I didn't hurt you."

"Yes, that's true. But I'm just..." she blushed, not sure how to finish her statement. "Well, let's just say that I'm not used to this form of exercise," she finished lamely.

He stood up, his features appearing almost mischievous as he paused beside the bed. "I have a cure for that," he told her, bending down and, a moment later, he lifted her into his arms, minus the sheet.

"Goran! What are you doing?" she demanded, trying to cover her naked breasts even while trying to hold onto him at the same time.

"Obviously you haven't explored the cabana that your brother arranged for us. There is a private pool just outside."

He pushed open one of the glass doors, leaving it to swish silently closed behind them.

"A pool?" she whispered, forgetting about trying to cover herself as the beauty of their surroundings hit her. There was indeed a pool. The water shimmered in the morning sunshine while dense foliage surrounded the edges of the stone patio. There were chaise lounges on the flat stones, but Goran wasn't heading in their direction. He walked towards the pool. "You're not...Goran, don't you dare!" she hissed. But he continued walking.

Thankfully, he walked to the end of the pool where the stairs were located, lowering them both into the cool water slowly.

"Did you think I was going to throw you in?" he asked, still holding her as the water swished around them.

Calista sighed, wrapping her arms around his neck as she smiled in relief. "I had no idea what you were going to do," she admitted. "You're a horrible man and..." The water swished around her. Calista sighed, relaxing into his embrace. "Well, let's face it. We don't really know each other."

He shrugged slightly, nodding his head as he moved towards the deeper end of the pool. "That's true enough," he replied, his tone conversational. "So why don't we rectify that?"

She leaned her head against his shoulder, enjoying the cool relief of the water. "Should we?" she asked. "Goodness, this is really nice. Yesterday was...a nightmare." He made a noise that Calista couldn't translate. She looked up at him, her hands tightening. "Let's just get through this nightmare," she answered. "What have you heard from my brother? Any updates?"

"Nothing," he replied, moving them around in the water. "I spoke to Astir last night and explained what we knew so far." He looked at her with an admonishing glace. "You certainly were no help. You fell asleep on the big bed and didn't even leave me much room."

Calista rolled her eyes. "I don't see dark circles under your eyes, indicating that you struggled to sleep."

"I just pulled you into my arms and took over the bed's real estate."

She laughed, feeling carefree for the moment. "Okay, so what's the next step?"

"Your brother already sent a team to come and retrieve the guards we left behind in the jungle. He'll see what his men can get out of those

73

guys. We'll check in after the initial interrogation."

He released her legs and Calista swam away, still facing him but lowering her body into the water. It felt incredibly good. As an added bonus, it was really nice to look at him.

"What's for breakfast?" she asked.

He shrugged, moving his arms in a wide arc to push the water back and forth. "Well, we can't eat in the resort dining room, and I don't think it would be a good idea to have the wait staff coming into the cabana. But...we could go out into the small village nearby to get some food supplies. Or we could order food off of the menu and have it delivered, and just ask the wait staff to leave everything outside the door."

She tilted her head. "Wouldn't that seem suspicious?" she asked.

"I'm sure lots of people order room service," he countered.

"True, but when I've ordered room service while traveling, I've always allowed the wait staff to push the cart into the room. I also have to sign the receipt."

"As far as the staff are concerned, we're honeymooners."

Her eyes widened. "Is that what my brother arranged?"

Goran shook his head. "Yes. When he and I talked yesterday, we both agreed that a couple honeymooning together would be a good cover. It won't appear strange to the staff who might normally come through the cabana to clean or deliver food. We thought it would be a good reason to keep everyone away. Also, the reservations were paid for from a distant account tied to a company that your brother owns, but it would be hard to track his ownership in that entity. We didn't want anything directly or indirectly connected to either of our governments."

"That's good, but then how are we going to get food?"

"I think we should order room service this morning. I don't know about you but I'm hungry enough that I'm not sure if I care who sees me."

"Me too," she agreed.

"Good. Then we give ourselves a break this morning and get room service. But after that, we go into town and get supplies."

"Is that safe? What if someone recognizes us?"

"We'll use hats and sunglasses to hide our features. And we'll be careful. We'll dress up to look like ordinary tourists."

She grinned. "So we'll be completely incognito?"

"Exactly," he replied with a matching smile.

"Sounds like a fun plan." She bit her lip, looking around to see where the towels were located.

"Towels are by the wall," he told her, reading her mind.

She looked at him, then over at the stack of fluffy white towels neatly stacked on a shelf. And yes, they were right outside the bedroom door-way. In order to get a towel, she'd have to walk out of the pool naked.

"You're doing it again," she replied, spying his lascivious grin.

"Hey," he lifted his hands, palms up. "I'm not stopping you. You're the one that is too self-conscious to get out and grab a towel."

She sighed, pushing her hair back. "I don't suppose that you would be a gentleman and get a towel for me."

He chuckled. "So you want me to get out of the water and allow you to survey my naked body, but you're unwilling to do the same?"

She considered his question, then nodded her head. "Yes. You're less self-conscious than I am. So yes, I'm more than willing to let you get out of the pool and grab a towel for me."

He laughed, throwing his head back as he pushed his dark hair over his head. "Fine," he replied, then moved over to the edge of the pool. With powerful movements, he lifted himself out of the water, then walked over to the stack of towels. He picked up two, lifting one to dry his face and he set the other one on the table. Several feet from the edge of the pool.

She groaned, eyeing him with laughing anger. "You're still going to make me get out of the water, aren't you?"

He nodded as he unfolded the towel and started to dry off. "You might as well get used to walking around me naked. We'll be seeing each other naked a lot over the next few days."

Calista groaned, frustration and nervousness hitting her as a dual impact. "Have I mentioned how horrible you are?" she grumbled. But a moment later, she walked over to the stairs. For a moment, she remained under the water and he shook his head. "You know I can see everything under the water right?"

She sighed with resignation. "No, I hadn't really thought about that," she replied, then stood up and, with as much dignity as possible, stepped out of the pool. She walked over to the towel and picked it up, then whipped it open so that she could cover herself with it.

He laughed, stepping closer to wrap a strong arm around her waist. "See? Was that so hard?' he asked.

Then he kissed her. It was another deep, soul searching, mind altering kiss, and she lifted onto her toes for more.

Chapter 7

The local market was teeming with people. Calista wasn't sure if that was good or bad, but she tugged her baseball cap down lower, covering more of her face. She'd pulled her hair into a band, keeping it in a ponytail because Goran warned her that her normal tight bun on the back of her neck would be too recognizable. Reluctantly, she'd left it down, even though the heat and humidity caused several strands to stick to her neck.

"What are you going to do with that?" Goran asked, peering over her shoulder when she examined different vegetables at the farmer's stand.

She shrugged and gave the man some of the money that had been delivered to their door by a messenger. "I'm not planning to do anything with it," she warned him, moving on to the next stand that was filled with various types of grains and breads.

"Do you have any idea how to cook with those ingredients?"

She shrugged and paid for a loaf of crusty bread. "I'm not cooking tonight," she told him. "You are." And with that, she moved on to the next area where she selected some pink fish. It wasn't salmon, she thought, but it looked delicious. It was currently chilling on ice, but thankfully, it had already been deboned.

"You're not seriously going to make me cook!" he warned, his voice telling her how outraged he was at the idea.

She looked at him over her shoulder. "Why wouldn't you cook?' she asked.

"Because..." he said, then stopped, his mind halting the potentially sexist flow of words, staring at her initially with stunned surprise, then with suspicion. Calista smiled smugly, recognizing exactly where he was going with his comments. "Fine," he finished with a jerk of his head. "Choose away." He waved his hand towards the various menu options. Only after a triumphant expression showed on her lovely features did he lean forward and whisper, "But tomorrow, I'm picking the ingredients and you'll be the one trying to figure out what to cook for our meals."

She laughed, delighted with the possibility. She had no idea how to cook, but the internet was a wonderful thing! "Sounds like an excellent plan!"

Goran stared at her as she walked over to the next stall, which was piled high with oranges and lemons, his eyes automatically taking in her adorable ass. The same ass that he'd cupped with his hands this morning as she'd moved over him, stroking his shaft with her body and making him groan with appreciation. She'd been so lovely this morning and...wait! What was she looking at now? She paid another market vendor and stuffed another strange ingredient into the fabric bag they'd bought when first entering the market.

Hurrying to catch up with her, he tried to peer into the bag. But Calista merely shifted, once again distracting him when her hand touched his chest. It took him several moments to get his sizzled brain back in gear after her casual touch.

By the time he did, she was standing in front of another market vendor, smiling and chatting in Spanish with the owner of a fruit stand.

"Calista, you're...!" he hurried after her, trailing less than a foot behind her. "Calista, what are you saying?" he asked.

Calista was having a marvelous time! The marketplace was a whole new world, and she loved the scents and sounds and colors! Everything was new and delightful! Everything sounded so chaotic as the vendors called out to potential customers, haggled about prices or simply chatted with friends and neighbors. And the colors! Goodness, Calista loved the colors! Every vendor vied to capture the eye with bright, vibrant signs, their roofs and support beams painted with bright oranges, yellows, greens, and various shades of blue!

She breathed in again, trying to identify the scents. Coffee was being brewed as well as sold. There was a small café on the side of the market where patrons sat on chairs, sipping the fragrant brew. Sacks of the beans were stacked up at several stalls, either as whole beans or, if the customer asked, ground for brewing convenience.

There were also herbs and spices, scents she couldn't identify, so she walked over to those vendors and bought several samples. She had no idea what she could do with the spices, but she was going to learn! Goodness, how had she not known about markets like this?

It was so far from the carefully organized and orchestrated world in which she lived, and Calista loved everything about it! Everything was so vital and alive!

And it was exciting to see the obvious discomfort in Goran's eyes when she selected the raw materials for their meals! Calista smothered her smile, keeping her eyes pointed away from Goran. She could hear the small bite of nervousness in his voice. "You're the one who said we needed to keep away from people as much as possible."

"Yes, but...!"

"And you're the one who said that we should get our foods from this marketplace." She turned, her face a picture of innocence. She blinked up at him, feigning worry. "Are you...you can't...!" she bit her lip, adding a bit of insecurity to her question. Lowering her voice, she placed a hand on his chest and sighed. "I thought you were such a superhero, Goran," she said softly to him, then slowly lifted her eyes to stare into his, hoping for a doe-eyed look of hope, tinged with a touch of doubt and fear. "I thought you were the kind of man who could figure anything out." Calista thought the small tremble in her voice was a nice touch. "When you knocked that guard down after the two of them drove up to that shack," she paused to shudder, shaking her head and briefly closing her eyes. When she opened them again, she added a small shiver, really getting into her role now. "You were my hero." She let her breath go slightly and started to turn away. "I thought you could do anything. I thought you could..."

For a moment, she had him fooled. He stared down at her, his mouth literally hanging open as he watched her performance. But Calista must have overplayed it, because his features changed, shifting from stunned horror to amused disdain.

"You're messing with me," he growled, snapping her body right back against his. "And you're going to pay for it."

It took all of her self-control to keep her features clear of the amusement brewing inside of her. "I don't understand."

He growled again under his breath as he grabbed her elbow, towing her out of the marketplace. Since he was no longer facing her, she smiled brightly, waving to the merchants as she passed back through the crowded stalls. He didn't stop until they were back at the Jeep and he lifted her into the passenger seat, slamming the door when she was safely inside.

While he walked around the front of the Jeep, his eyes surveying the crowd for danger even now, she couldn't hold back a snort of laughter. This really was a cruel trick, but...she was in the mood for some fun!

He slipped inside the Jeep and grunted when he started the engine. "Tell me what you want me to make."

She threw back her head, laughing at his disgruntled expression as he swung the Jeep out of the packed dirt area that was used as a parking lot for the marketplace. "I would never smother your creativity by telling you what to cook, Goran! You're a very intelligent man," she continued, resting her elbow on the edge of the open window and lifting her face up for the breeze as they drove back to the resort. "I know that you can come up with something brilliant for dinner."

"You're messing with me, Calista," he told her, his voice clear and firm. "And you know I will get payback in some way."

She grinned, leaning back in her seat. "Well, I'm not afraid of you."

"You should be," he replied smoothly, shifting into a higher gear as he turned onto the highway.

Calista's only response was a light laugh, feeling relaxed and free!

Chapter 8

"Goran?" Calista called out, smoothing her hands back and forth in the clear water of their private pool. She sniffed the air. It was still clean and earthy, with a hint of the salt in the pool, but there was something else. Something that smelled...off. "Something is burning!"

There'd been a clattering of pans and puffs of smoke coming from their small kitchenette for the past hour. She'd also heard a few muttered expletives, but she'd merely ignored all of it as she read her book. When Calista had become too hot, she'd slipped into the water to cool off.

"This is the life," she whispered, closing her eyes as she took another sip of the chilled white wine she'd poured herself earlier.

"What's the life?" Goran demanded, stepping through one of the sliding glass doors to the stone patio. He sat down in one of the patio chairs, a cold beer in his hand. Unfortunately, a whole wardrobe of clothing had been delivered earlier this morning, so Goran was now wearing a pair of navy blue board shorts. Thankfully, he'd disdained a shirt, so Calista's eyes were free to roam over his broad, muscular chest.

Calista pulled her eyes away from him, afraid of becoming addicted to the sight of him. And his touch. And his scent. As soon as this kidnapping issue was resolved, she and Goran would go back to their real lives. And all of the beautiful touches and sighs and the lovely pleasure of just being with him would die away, just as it had during their engagement.

"This," she replied, answering his question with a sigh as she swirled around in the pool. "No public appearances. No comments on some vicious person's social media page about how I've gained five pounds or I look pale or," she groaned, "pregnancy speculation."

"That happens?" he asked, his whole body tightening with anger on her behalf.

"Of course it happens," she replied. "Women especially are vicious. You'd think that we'd learn how to be gentle with our comments because we know how much they can hurt. But we don't."

"Why is that?"

Calista shrugged. "I don't know. I don't go on social media anymore, although I hear about the comments when I read the news. So I don't know exactly who is saying the comments about my weight or my hair or the cut of my suit or whether I cross my legs in a lady-like fashion or if I accidentally show a bit too much thigh when I get out of a vehicle." She sighed and visibly relaxed. "I don't know who says those comments, but I know they are repeated in the media and online."

There was a long silence, but Calista could hear him thinking even when she was on the other side of the pool.

"Is that why you appear so tense when you're out in public?" he finally asked.

She smiled, but didn't bother to open her eyes. "Yes. It's miserable. Being a public figure, but without any other official responsibilities, is tough." She shifted her arms and looked at him. "If I had some sort of public job, then I could lose myself in that persona. I can handle someone criticizing my ideas. I can change my mind, or I can incorporate someone else's opinion into my ideas." She shifted in the water. "What I can't do is lose weight instantly. I can't make my hair look perfect when it is one hundred and thirty degrees outside and I'm wearing a long sleeve silk blouse underneath a long-sleeved suit jacket. It's hot," she said. "And I can't change the color of my makeup as quickly as I can change my outfit, even when I try to choose similar colors for all of the events to which I'm scheduled to appear during the day."

He stared at her for a long moment until Calista finally turned around, stepping out of the pool. She grabbed a towel to dry off, covering herself despite the relatively conservative bathing suit she'd donned. Grabbing her glass of wine, she took a long sip, trying to release the stress that had accumulated in her shoulders during that tirade.

"Sorry," she said when she sat down in the chair opposite him. "I know it's silly of me to whine when I have literally every advantage. But some of the comments people write about me are hard to take."

"I can't imagine what you go through," he said softly.

Calista shook her head as she took another sip of her wine. "Don't feel sorry for me, Goran," she told him firmly. "I'm a princess. I've traveled to places that others would only dream of seeing. I've had incredible experiences and learned languages and had private tutors. If there was something I wanted to do, then I should have stepped forward to do it."

"But we live in a male dominated society. Because you're a princess, you're a role model. If you stepped out of your role, then you would be subject to even harsher criticism."

She bowed her head for a moment contemplatively, then lifted her eyes to stare back at him. "That's what I used to think," she finally replied. "Then I met Rachel, my new sister-in-law. She had Astir jumping through hoops prior to their wedding date. And even after, she is brilliant. She never takes any of his sexist crap. She ignores everyone's opinions and just does what she does best. He told her that she wouldn't be able to continue her lifestyle vlogging business after the wedding. But the woman is brilliant at coming up with new ideas for people to do at home, ways to make their worlds better or prettier. She ignored my brother and just did her thing." Calista sighed and looked out at the dense foliage. "Rachel could have relaxed and lived the life of a pampered wife." She snorted. "Astir tends to spoil her until she tells him to stop." She smiled slightly, shaking her head. "And even after she tells him to stop, he continues with small, lovely gifts, all of which are personally selected by my older brother in order to make her happy." She laughed. "It's quite startling to watch them together."

"You get along well with your younger sister?"

Calista nodded. "Yeah. It was Ayla and me against Astir for years!' She laughed, thinking back to previous pranks. "We loved it when he came back from university."

"Why is there such an age difference between you and your brother?"

Her smile faded and she shrugged one shoulder. "My mother got very sick after giving birth to Astir. After that nightmare, my father refused to let her get pregnant again until she laid down the law. But it took her another few years after that to convince him that she was strong enough to have more children."

"And Rachel? Is her pregnancy okay?"

Calista nodded, thinking back. "Rachel is a strong, powerful woman! Astir kept trying to get her to sit down and take things easy during her pregnancy. But Rachel refused, telling him that pregnancy was a normal part of life and not a disease."

"Still, pregnancy is hard on a woman's body."

"Yes, it's very hard. But it's also a gift."

"You want children?" he asked softly.

Calista smiled, nodding slowly. "Yes. Eventually. I'd like a large family. Lots of kids."

He opened his mouth to reply, but the kitchen buzzer went off, indicating that something had finished cooking in the small kitchen. "I'll be right back," he told her, standing up and going through the glass doors to investigate.

Calista sat there, staring at the water and wondering why she'd revealed so much to Goran. Rubbing her forehead, she shook her head. He probably didn't care.

But...the expression in his eyes...he'd looked as if...he might care? Just a little?

Calista walked along the stone patio and dried off, grabbing the cover-up that had arrived with the rest of her clothes.

No, this time with him, isolated from the world...these crazy, special few days together wasn't the real world. Goran had been distant and distracted before they'd been kidnapped. He hadn't had time for her back then. She was fooling herself to think that he might care for her now.

Besides, after seeing how Astir loved Rachel, the way they doted on each other, cared for each other deeply and discovered small ways to show their love for each other every day...Calista wanted that from her husband. She didn't want a marriage that was simply a business transaction or political merger.

That had been another reason why she'd wanted to break off her engagement. She'd wanted what her brother had with Rachel.

Goran came out of the cabana carrying two plates and set them down on the table. But before Calista could even look at what he'd prepared, Goran took her hands and pulled her out of the chair, right into his arms. She thudded against his hard chest with a soft sound that was instantly absorbed by his mouth.

He was kissing her? Calista was shocked for perhaps half a second. Then the reality of this moment caught up with her and she lost herself in the beauty of that kiss. It was magical and, coming on the heels of their very personal conversation and thoughts of the way Astir and Rachel treated each other, she let herself become swept up in the kiss.

Opening her mouth, she leaned into him, exploring him with her mouth and her hands, loving the way he cradled her against him.

But that kiss was over too soon and he pulled back, looking down at her. "You're worth it," he said softly, his deep voice gruff and sounding sincere.

Calista licked her lips, slowly pulling out of his arms. "Thank you," she whispered, wishing that her voice sounded more confident.

"Let's eat," he said, stepping back and gesturing to the plates filled with food.

Calista looked down at the table, her eyes widening at the amount of food he'd prepared. The fish she'd selected was...cooked! It was a bit black around the edges, but the bulk of the fish looked edible! There was also a salad and toasted bread. It wasn't an elaborate meal, but it actually smelled...good!

"You...cooked this?" she asked, sitting down and spreading the linen napkin over her lap.

"Of course I cooked it," he replied, sitting down as well and picking up his fork. But he didn't take a bite. Instead, he waited until she'd sampled the fish. "What do you think?" he asked.

Calista braced herself for something horrible. But as the garlic and wine marinade hit her taste buds, she had to admit that she was pleasantly surprised! "This is actually...good!" she gasped, taking another bite. "You got this recipe off of the internet and just...cooked it?"

He took a bite of the fish himself, nodding. "Of course I cooked it," he repeated. "I had to watch a few other videos. I wasn't exactly sure how to turn on the oven," he confessed, an exasperated expression on his rough features. "But once that was figured out, it was easy enough. The sauce isn't very elaborate. I just used oil, vinegar, white wine and garlic with a few herbs but..."

"Wait a minute, where did you get those ingredients?" she demanded.

He looked sheepish for a moment, but he rallied quickly. "I called someone in the resort kitchen to deliver some additional ingredients. They left them in a basket beside the door." When she started to argue that he'd cheated, he held up his hand. "Seriously, there was no way I could make anything with just the ingredients that you bought from the market. And since you'll have to reciprocate tomorrow night, and I'm choosing the ingredients, then let me get away with this small issue so that you'll have a chance tomorrow as well."

Calista hadn't thought of that, so instead of berating him for cheating, she stabbed another bite of the fish and continued eating. He merely grinned, then dug into his food as well.

"Just find them!" Ned snapped. "And find them fast! The location I gave you should have been secure enough that no one could have escaped!"

Petro Zinhaden silently stepped into the tent, almost snorting when he overheard the conversation. He didn't know the details, but had heard through his own sources that the Sheik of Skyla was potentially missing along with Princess Calista del Taran. Petro hadn't known why the sheik had disappeared until now.

So...Ned, the idiot, had kidnapped a world leader of a powerful country. Interesting. Stupid, but interesting.

Why the hell would the man take such a monumental risk? And did he have a plan B now that the sheik was no longer missing?

"They have to still be in the country. I have people stationed at the airport and they haven't left. The man is trained in survival methods. He's probably hunkered down somewhere with that bitch, waiting for a rescue team to get to him. Find the man before his people do or we're all in trouble!"

When Ned ended the call with an irritated snap, his nemesis, Petro, didn't bother to leave the worksite tent. Ned turned around and spotted Petro standing in the "entry", he couldn't hide the startled look in his eyes. "What the hell are you doing here?"

Petro shrugged and moved forward. "Just letting you know that..."

"Hey boss," Scott Roland interrupted. Both men turned, scowling at the shorter man. Of the three men that Neville had put in charge here, Scott was the least threatening. The man was a weeny, Petro thought. Probably a bit pathetic to boot. The guy drank most of the time and only ventured towards the drilling operations occasionally to boss a few people around and pretend that he added value to the growing mess that was this drilling effort.

Boy, when old man Neville had hired these idiots, he'd probably thought he'd gotten the cream of the crop of the underworld. Obviously not!

There was one thing that Scott could do well though. He was excellent at reading a room. Or a tent, Petro thought.

"Sorry!" Scott said, lifting his hands in the air and offering a small chuckle. "I've interrupted something here. I'll come back later."

A moment later, Scott left the tent and Petro turned back to Ned.

"What the hell do you want?" Ned snapped.

Petro smothered his amusement and that only irritated Ned further.

Petro lifted his hands in the air. "Nothing. Just letting you know that the drills have reached the efiasia deposit. The extraction teams have moved in and are starting that phase of the operation."

Finally, some good news! "Okay. Fine," he said dismissively. When Petro didn't take the hint, Ned glared at the goon, correctly interpreting his continued presence as a threat to his authority. That realization was compounded when Petro simply gave the other man a slow, annoying smile, then, finally, turned and walked out of the tent.

Ned heard Petro whistling as he walked back to the massive hole in the ground that the mammoth drills had created. The hole was covered by a huge tarp scattered with desert brush so the satellites couldn't detect the operation. As Ned watched the former KGB officer stroll away, he wondered if the tarps and brush were enough. He had a sneaking suspicion that it wasn't.

Chapter 9

Calista stared at the pile of food on the small countertop, her mind trying to take it all in but a niggling sensation of panic grew inside of her.

Goran stepped into the cabana, wiping off the water from the pool.

Calista turned her eyes towards him, glaring at the man. "What's all of this?" she asked, waving her hand over the pile. There were fruits, vegetables, odd-looking grains, small bottles of oil, vinegar and some spices.

"That is your meal challenge for tonight," he told her, walking over and kissing her neck before heading into the bathroom to shower.

"But...!"

He turned, his dark eyes brightening with amusement. "Payback, my dear," he told her, then disappeared.

She turned and stared down at the food. "I hadn't planned on this kind of payback," she muttered under her breath.

"What kind of payback were you anticipating?" he asked, sliding in behind her.

Calista had thought he'd gone into the bathroom and that she was alone! His voice caused her to jump in surprise. "I thought you were in the shower!" she exclaimed, peering at him over her shoulder.

"I was, but then I forgot this," he said, turning her around and pulling her into his arms. Calista protested for perhaps half a second. But then his mouth moved over hers and she was lost once again to the magic of his kisses.

When he lifted his mouth, they were clinging to each other. "What do you think you might make?" he asked, sliding his hands along her waist, stopping just under her breasts.

Calista opened her mouth, trying to reply. But in her mind, all she could think about were his hands...so close!

"No idea," she replied honestly.

"There's some chicken in the fridge."

"Ah!" she moaned, but was that because of his announcement about the chicken? Or the fact that his big, strong hands were now cupping her breasts. When his thumb flicked over her nipple, she didn't care! Her whole mind was focused on those thumbs and what he might do next.

"The resort also sent over some flour and sugar and a few spices," he told her, his neck bending so that his lips could nibble on her neck.

"That's good," she whispered, leaning her head over to the right so that his lips could tease the skin there.

"I'll even be generous and teach you how to use the oven."

"Ah!" Once again, that sound was all she could manage.

He laughed softly, then spun her around. Calista gasped, startled by the move. But his hands slid down her arms, holding her hands as he carefully, slowly, placed her palms flat on the countertop.

"I don't think you're paying a great deal of attention to the dinner possibilities."

She almost smiled, but he leaned against her, the wet bathing suit he had on was now pressed against her derriere. But she didn't care about the bathing suit or the wetness. Her mind was only paying attention to the long, enticing erection now evident against her back.

Calista wiggled, trying to tell him to hurry up.

"I was going to shower."

She made a protesting sound, then pressed her bottom against that throbbing erection, silently begging him to change his plans.

She sighed with relief when she felt his warm hands slide underneath her shirt. A moment later, that piece of clothing was whipped off, out of the way.

"Bend over, *habibi*," he urged, pressing a hand to her back between her shoulder blades.

"What?" she whispered, looking at him over her shoulder.

"Trust me," he soothed, his hands moving to her breasts once more, those thumbs doing things to her nipples that she couldn't fight.

Blindly, Calista leaned over. She felt his fingers move down her stomach, sliding underneath the waistband of her shorts and his fingers felt so good! She couldn't stifle the moan as his fingers slipped underneath the lace of her panties.

Goran hadn't meant for this to get so out of hand, but as his fingers teased her soft, wet folds, he couldn't pull away. She was just so hot, so ready for him! And if she didn't stop pressing her soft ass against his shaft, he wasn't sure if he'd be able to control himself! She just felt so damn good!

"Just like that!" she urged as his thumb pressed against that nub, finding a rhythm that caused her hips to shift, pressing against his fingers. But that wasn't enough. Not this time! He wanted to be inside of her when she climaxed this time. He had to remember to pull out though.

Deftly, his fingers unsnapped the button on her shorts, letting them drop to the ground. He wished that he could concentrate enough to get rid of her panties, but at this point, he just...couldn't. A tearing sound echoed throughout the room and he tossed the scrap of lace to the side.

"Goran?" she whispered, trying to see him over her shoulder.

"Relax, *habibi*," he soothed, running his hands over her back again. She had the most beautiful back! But he needed to be inside of her. He needed to thrust into her and feel those muscles clench around him. He shifted, tossing his bathing suit off to the side, then coming back to stand behind Calista. "Bend over slightly," he told her, but put his hands on her back when she didn't move fast enough for him. Then his hands moved back around to her stomach, holding her in place while he teased her opening with his shaft. She was so wet, so hot and ready for him.

"Tell me if I hurt you," he warned, then thrust into her heat.

Calista threw her head back, stiffening slightly and Goran stilled, worried that he'd pushed too hard. But a moment later, she wiggled, her body shifting, accepting his shaft into her heat.

"More," she groaned, bending forward more in an effort to take all of him into her body. When she wiggled again, Goran grabbed her hips, slowing her down. One of his hands moved to her hair, his fingers fisting in the long, messy tresses. She looked well and truly loved, her mouth open, her eyes closed and her head back as if she wanted him to do more. So he did and Calista wiggled again. And again! Damn, he was going to lose control if she didn't stop that!

"I need...more," she whispered, her hands moving from the countertop to his thighs, her nails digging into the skin there while she pressed back against him.

"Relax," he said again.

She shook her head and Goran almost laughed. She was so tight, so ready for him, he nearly went cross-eyed as her body responded to his every thrust. Again and again, he moved into her with his erection while his free hand moved lower, rubbing that nub with the same rhythm. He knew what she needed and watched her face, trying to anticipate what she was feeling, how close she was getting to her own climax. He needed her to go first because, from experience, he wouldn't last much longer after she exploded. It was just too erotic and her body was too tight, too perfect. She felt too good. Hell, just thinking about her climaxing was bringing him closer to that precipice.

He used two fingers now, sliding against the edges of her nub then coming to rub the top and the sides, moving around to tease her on all sides. He could feel her fingernails biting into his thighs and loved the sensation, his hand tightening around her hair. He released her hair but only to tweak her nipple, pinching and teasing, tweaking it slightly and then pinching it a bit harder, bringing her closer and closer. Her cries were making him crazy and he increased the pressure with his fingers, needing to bring her over the edge so he could let himself go.

When she finally cried out, her body bent lower and one of her hands slapped over his, guiding him and that was so hot, so unexpected, he couldn't hold back any longer. He thrust into her, her hand still holding his in place, showing him what she needed while his body exploded in an intense climax, her own pleasure milking him until they were both panting, their bodies still poised as if neither of them were sure what had just happened.

Goran pulled her closer, cradling her in his arms. She wiggled around and he lifted her up, setting her down on the counter. She hissed slightly, as her bare skin connected with the cool granite of the counter-top, but he merely kissed her, soothing the ache.

"That was incredible," she whispered into his mouth, kissing him again and again as their bodies slowly relaxed. She smiled, he laughed. Calista kissed his neck, as if she needed to bury her face against him, hiding from him. Goran didn't mind. She was...beautiful. In so many ways, he was finding new ways that she pleasured him. Not just sexually, although...he almost laughed again at how much she'd pleasured him sexually!

"You're just trying to get out of cooking, aren't you?" he teased.

Calista jerked backwards, gasping in outrage. "*You* interrupted *me!*" she asserted firmly, tapping him on his bare shoulder as if to punish him.

"A likely excuse," he replied with a triumphant grin.

Calista laughed, but she jumped down off of the countertop. "Go away," she grumbled. "I have some cooking to do and..." She looked around, searching for her panties. "What did you do?" she demanded when she picked up the tattered piece of lace.

He took the bits out of her hand, tossing them into the garbage. "A casualty of your passion."

She laughed, picking up her shorts. She pulled them on over her nakedness, but Goran knew she'd go into the bedroom and grab another pair of panties. Calista wasn't a prude, but she didn't like going commando. Pity, he thought as he moved back into the bedroom to shower.

He came out a few minutes later to find Calista watching a video about...making cookies? They didn't have a laptop, but the resort television connected to the internet for guests. It was simple to see what she was watching and he wanted to laugh.

"Cookies?" he asked, coming over to hug her and kiss her neck.

Distractedly, she kissed him back, but quickly turned back to the television to listen intently. "Go away! I'm not letting you distract me again," she told him firmly.

Goran stopped on his way towards the table where he'd left his cell phone, looking back at her. She must have sensed his look because she glanced over at him. She started to turn back to the television and the tutorial, but one look at his determined expression and she laughed. A split second later, she was running across the cabana with Goran in hot pursuit. It took him less than three steps to capture her and she screamed, laughing as he tossed her over his shoulder.

"Oh, you think that you can give me orders, eh?" he teased, bending so that he could nibble on that spot below her ear that he now knew was extremely ticklish.

"I'm sorry!" she yelled, laughing and gasping for breath. "I'm sorry!"

"That's better," he growled, but kept her in his arms as he kissed her for another long moment. Putting her down, he spanked her bottom lightly. "Still trying to get out of dinner, I see."

Calista laughed, delighted with the man as she walked back to her place on the couch, pressing the rewind button so she could watch the missed instructions on the cookie baking video. "You're horrible," she grumbled.

Goran laughed as he picked up his phone and dialed Astir. For the next forty minutes, he and Astir discussed the latest information on speaker phone so that Calista could hear while she mixed and scooped and did odd things to what he suspected was cookie dough. But when she pulled the stuff out of the oven the first time, there were just hard, black disks. She tapped them with a ragged fingernail, then scraped everything into the trash. With a sigh, she put more blobs onto the cookie sheet while Goran listened to Astir discuss something about a mining company. It wasn't the same mining company that had given him pause. He didn't recognize the company name.

That captured Calista's attention and she paused, a spoon halted in mid-air as she lifted a finger.

"Wait!" Calista called out.

Goran's eyes lifted to hers, then he said, "Hold on just a second," just as her brother started to say something. Goran lifted dark eyebrows, silently prompting her to continue.

"Sorry for interrupting," she said, feeling her cheeks heat up. "But I think I heard someone at an event recently talk about a staging something or other near your border."

"What was it about?"

Calista bowed her head, trying to remember. "I don't think I can recite the whole conversation. It was one of those really boring events and I just wanted to get out of there as fast as possible. But she was saying something about big trucks and..." she blinked, looking up at Goran. "At the time, I hadn't thought anything about it. I know that we had some trouble with a mining company doing illegal digging that had collapsed a town. But that was in Silar. Not in Skyla."

"Think, Calista," Astir urged through the phone. "What did the woman say?"

She bit her lip, trying to concentrate. "She wasn't specific. Just something about...big trucks." She lifted her eyes again. "Could that have something to do with a mining company too?"

Goran nodded. "I had a request for a mining permit that has been niggling at the back of my mind. I don't remember any details, but the permit request might have been for an area towards my northern border. I didn't think about it before because," he paused, shaking his head. "Well, I want to say that the mining request would cover territory not just in Sklya, but also in Citran. I'll have my agency look into that detail and I'll have him call you. I'll ask him to call both of us with any additional information."

"If there's trouble brewing even close to Citran, then we should loop Zantar in on the issue," he commented, referring to Sheik Zantar al Abouss, the man who ruled Citran. He was a big brute of a guy, smart and an excellent ruler. "I'll check in with Zantar to find out if he's heard anything recently. Then I'll put that information together with the rest of what we've learned and will update you when we know something more," Astir replied.

"Tell Zantar that he owes me from our last poker game." The two men laughed, then he continued, "We'll wait for your call."

He clicked off and Calista continued dumping blobs onto the cookie sheet.

"Are those...?" Goran asked, peering down at the gooey blobs.

She sighed, lifting the tray and putting it into the small oven. "I'm hoping this batch turn out to be edible cookies," she explained. "I'm not sure what I did wrong the last time."

Goran walked over to the oven, his eyes narrowing. "Is there a difference between broiling and...?"

Calista gasped. "Yes!" she said and rushed over, taking the cookie sheet out again. "Darn it! Broiling is bad, according to one of the videos." She pressed a few more buttons. "There," she said, with a nod. "It's on bake now." She then turned and started mixing the dough, scraping it down off the sides of the large bowl.

Goran leaned against the wall, watching her carefully. "Are you...enjoying this?" he asked, stunned and...kind of turned on!

She stopped mixing for a moment, turning to look at him. Her features were still for a long moment, then her face broke out into a big smile and she laughed. "Yeah!" She paused again, stunned by this realization. "Yeah, I'm really enjoying this baking thing." She gestured to the fruit salad that was sitting on the counter, ready for their dinner. "I mixed up a lime dressing for the fruit and..." she laughed, shaking her head, "I am intrigued by all of this cooking stuff."

She started mixing again, intent on her efforts. "For so long, I've merely eaten food prepared by some mysterious person. My food was delivered to the dining room and simply set down in front of me. I never had any say in what foods were served or how they were prepared." She stirred briskly, her arm muscles visible now. "Our little..." she rolled her eyes, "...adventure has caused me to try my hand at different life skills, such as cooking, that I didn't even know would be interesting." She looked at him over her shoulder. "That whole drugging and kidnapping thing wasn't fun. But I liked kicking the other men down and helping you tie them up. Traipsing through the jungle was pretty fun too, as was reading a map and figuring out where we were. All very useful skills."

Goran couldn't stop himself. Not after those revelations. He walked over to her and pulled her into his arms. For a long moment, he simply held her, absorbing her feminine strength and reveling in the beauty of who she was.

"I didn't like the kidnapping and drugging thing either," he finally said, "but I'm glad that you were with me. If it weren't for you and your brilliant shoes, we'd probably still be tied up in that pathetic treehouse shack." Then he kissed her. It wasn't a romantic kiss; it was a kiss of... gratitude. Towards a woman? He almost laughed at how sexist his thoughts were. But then he kissed her again and...!

The buzzer went off, indicating that another batch of cookies were done.

Calista jerked out of his arms, rushing over to the oven to peer inside. "Oh, these look good!" she declared, stuffing her hand into an oven mitt before reaching into the oven to pull out...perfectly browned cookies!

"Extraordinary!" he replied, his mouth watering for a whole different reason now. "Can we eat them?"

Both of them were peering down at the rapidly cooling cookies as if they were some sort of miracle. "I think so!" she whispered. She slid the plastic spatula underneath one of the cookies, sliding it onto a plate. "They're supposed to cool off on some sort of wire thing but I couldn't find anything like that here in this small kitchen."

She started to take another cookie off the baking sheet but Goran picked up the warm cookie with his bare hands, taking a bite. "Wow!" he muttered, then took another bite. "It's warm and soft and...wow!"

Her anxious expression shifted to one of hope. "They're good?" she asked, a tinge of concern in her voice.

"They're awesome!" he replied. "I didn't know cookies could be eaten warm like this!"

Calista stopped and took a bite out of another cookie, then gasped. "Oh wow! You're right!"

"Give me another!" he demanded.

Calista shook her head, handing him the spatula while she stepped out of the way in order to eat her own warm cookie.

Goran slipped the spatula carefully under another cookie, his movements careful and precise. He treated each cookie as if it were a precious thing before taking a bite, closing his eyes and savoring the warm, gooey goodness. "You're a miracle worker," he commented, his mouth full and he reached over to pull her into his arms, kissing her even though his mouth was full. "Do more!" he ordered when he lifted his head, his arm still around her waist.

Calista laughed, delighted with both his admiration for her newly acquired skill as well as this affectionate, snuggly side of the man. Before this ordeal, Calista never would have suspected that Goran was a snuggly kind of person.

Thinking about that, she realized that she hadn't thought of herself as very snuggly either! She and Ayla hugged a great deal, but Astir...well, in Calista's mind, Astir was about as snuggly as a rock! He was big and muscular and sometimes annoyingly protective. But he was also much older than she and Ayla. She loved him, but they didn't hug often.

That was something she'd like to change, she thought, looking over at Goran who was concentrating on getting another cookie off of the cookie sheet. She laughed, rolling her eyes at him.

"What?" he growled, walking by her with his fourth cookie in his hand. He kissed the top of her head as he walked over to the television where he picked up the remote to find a movie to watch.

"You're not going to be hungry for dinner tonight," she called out to him, sneaking another cookie herself.

"I will be," he called right back. "What's your favorite movie?"

Calista stopped, her hands frozen as she looked at him. She could only see the back of his head since the sofa was facing the television, just as the kitchen did. But she saw him flipping through the channels, trying to find something in the ...romantic comedy category?

Her heart melted a bit more. "You don't need to watch a rom com," she told him, trying to hide the tenderness she felt from coming out in her voice.

He turned his head around so that he could look at her. "You watched one of my movies last night. And besides, I'd like to know what you enjoy watching."

Calista shivered, thinking that his eyes were lethal. "There's a movie called *Willow* that I've watched over and over," she told him.

He moved, turning so that he was almost facing her instead of just his face. "*Willow*? The one about a magical baby?"

"Yes," Calista admitted, bracing herself for ridicule. "I love that movie."

Goran noticed a tension in her now. Her jaw poked out a bit more and her eyes dared him to...what? Make fun of her movie preference?

He stood up and came over to her, ignoring the cookies because Calista was hurting for some reason. "Hey," he said softly, his thumb sliding against her tense jawline. "What's going on?"

Her chin jutted up a notch. "I'm just waiting."

"For what?"

Her lashes lowered, hiding her eyes from his view. "For you to tell me what a silly movie it is."

Goran hesitated for a long moment, then gave in to his instincts. Pulling her into his arms, he held her gently. Again, it wasn't a sexual embrace, and he was starting to marvel at his need to touch this woman all the time, even platonically.

"I don't think that the movie is silly, Calista," he told her gently. "Let's grab some real food," he tilted his head towards the fruit salad sitting on the counter, "pull up the movie and just relax for the rest of the evening?"

Calista relaxed, her body almost sagging at his lack of ridicule over her movie choice. "That sounds really nice."

They filled up plates with grilled chicken that he helped to season and roast in the oven, as well as the green salad and mixed fruit that she cut up and tossed. They both took their plates over and sat on the sofa. Goran was a typical male that evening. After eating their meal, he pulled her close, but retained control of the remote. They watched *Wil-*

low, a magical movie about saving a small baby girl who would eventually save the world. Calista loved the movie because of the romantic plot twists and Goran enjoyed the movie for the fight scenes, grunting appreciatively at the sword fights and gruesome explosions of trolls.

Throughout the movie, Goran kept his non-remote-holding arm around her, keeping her by his side. Calista leaned her head against his shoulder, enjoying the movie more than ever, simply because she was sharing it with this man.

When the movie ended, Calista turned her head towards Goran and he kissed her. And he didn't stop kissing her. When he lifted her into his arms and carried her into the bedroom, he didn't stop. When he laid her down on the covers, he continued. When he stripped off all of their clothes, he continued kissing her, touching every inch of newly bared skin. He kissed her mouth, her breasts, her stomach, her core...and continued kissing her until she screamed out with pleasure. And he kissed his way back up her body, kissing her as he entered her with almost painful slowness. It was pure lovemaking and Calista trembled as he brought her to pleasure, found his own, then continued clinging to him well into the night as they fell asleep in each other's arms.

Chapter 10

Calista jerked awake when a strong hand covered her mouth. "It's just me," she heard Goran whisper into her ear.

She tried to look at him, but he held her still. "Someone's here," he warned her.

All of the tension of the previous days came right back to her muscles. She looked around and Goran's hand slowly pulled away, ready to cover her mouth again if her nerves overcame common sense. She might have hissed at him that she wasn't that stupid, but decided to tell him that after they dealt with whoever was sneaking into their cabana.

Goran held up his hand, fingers spread wide, indicating that he thought there were five people so far. Calista nodded her understanding, grabbing the tee shirt and shorts he handed her. She didn't bother with underwear as she slipped to the other side of the bed. Moments later, both of them were dressed and ready, although neither of them had a weapon.

Calista could feel her heart thrumming against her ribs, but kept her head down, slowing her breathing so she could gain control of her senses. She knew from experience that raging emotions were the worst thing to have when one was confronted with a tense situation.

Goran tapped her shoulder and she looked at him. The darkness hid his features, but she could make out his hand lift into the air. He gestured to her that he was going to walk around to the other side of the room via the bathroom, trying to get behind whoever was coming in to attack. Calista nodded her understanding, looking around, trying to find some way to defend them. Five against two. Horrible odds, but then again, she had Goran on her side. Maybe the odds were pretty even, if not in their favor.

Calista shifted so that she was on her toes, ready to move as soon as she figured out where the threat would enter. When she saw a shadow in the corner, she stiffened, looked around and saw a pillow. Now she had a plan!

Taking the pillow from the floor where it had tumbled, most likely from their very active night activities, she clutched it with her fingers. When the man looked to the left, Calista threw the pillow to the right. The man, at least, she assumed it was a man, turned in the direction of the pillow, searching the corner of the room. That's when Calista attacked. As silently as possible, she sprinted across the room and leapt onto the man's back. With her arm wrapped around his neck, she squeezed with both her arms around the man's neck as he tried to knock her off of him. But Calista only squeezed harder, tightening her arm and started counting out the seconds. After only ten seconds, the man slowed down and, stumbling slightly, tumbling to the floor. Lack of oxygen did it every time, she thought, stepping away from the now-prone intruder. Moments later, she bent and unplugged the light from the socket, using the light's cord to tie the man's hands. She couldn't see well enough to tie off the ends to something substantial that would further immobilize the man, but the bound wrists would have to do for now.

The moment she finished tying the man up, another dark shadow appeared in the doorway of the bedroom. His first glance was to the bed where he expected both Calista and Goran to be. His next was to the corner of the room where she was hiding behind a very unsteady chair. Hopefully, the shadows would hide her from his view, but she pressed her back to the wall, just in case.

Again, she breathed as slowly as possible, wanting to hide the sound of her rapid breathing from whoever was trying to attack them. Thankfully, the man didn't see her, but he came deeper into the room. She guessed that the newest man had come to check on his teammate, who should have had both her and Goran pinned down already. But with the bed empty and no sign of the other man, the newest member of the attack team moved into the bathroom. This man had a weapon and Calista searched the downed man for anything else she could use against this next intruder.

Thankfully, she found both a pistol as well as a knife. She tucked the pistol in one hand and shifted the knife around so that it was facing downward. She didn't have as much upper body strength, so her security team had taught her to use her body weight. When the newest guy moved to the other side of the bed, Calista moved right behind him. She felt only slightly squeamish when she plunged the knife into the man's arm. She should have stabbed him in the back, but she simply couldn't do it. She figured the man's gun arm was the next best solution.

When the man ground out a muffled curse, Calista jerked the man around, sweeping his feet out from under him and twisting his other arm around until he was face down on the ground. Once he was down she kicked the knife wound. The man groaned in pain, but Calista didn't pay any attention to him. She stuffed part of the sheet around his mouth, gagging him and preventing him from warning the others. She used the knife again to cut the remainder of the sheet up so she could bind the man's hands, unconcerned about the bleeding wound in his upper arm. She'd take care of that wound once the sun came up.

Seconds later, Goran burst into the room, flipping on the lights. Calista blinked, startled by the sudden light and looked around. Her eyes moved over Goran, searching for any wounds. There was a minor scratch on his cheek, but otherwise, he seemed to be intact.

"Are you okay?" Goran demanded, stepping into the room carrying two automatic rifles slung over his chest as well as a pistol in one hand and a knife in the other. His eyes quickly moved over her, doing the same search as she'd just done.

"I'm fine," she told him, standing up and looking around as if searching for another attacker. "You're hurt."

Goran looked at the two men, both of whom were tied up, and his mouth dropped open. "What the hell happened in here?"

Calista laughed, then moved over to lean against him, the adrenaline rushing out of her system now. "I'm not just a pretty face," she told him, trying to get him to smile. But he didn't laugh. Instead, he wrapped his arms around her, pulling her hard against his chest. He buried his face against her neck, breathing in her scent as if he needed that as confirmation that she was unharmed.

"I was so worried when I couldn't find two of the attackers. I knew they were coming in here and...!" His arms tightened and Calista could barely breathe for a moment, but she didn't say anything to him. Instead, she let him hold her, feeling safe and secure despite the two men sitting on the floor, one of whom was twisting around, fighting his restraints. Goran kicked him and Calista wasn't sure if he'd meant to aim directly for the wound on the man's arm.

Goran pulled back, looking down at her. "I think our little vacation is over," he said. "We were hiding out here, but I don't think that our efforts were very successful." He sighed, leaning his forehead against hers. "We need to go home. We need to get back and figure this out ourselves. I'm pretty sure that someone in my government is the inside person, but I won't know who until I'm there to investigate." He kissed her temple and pulled her close again. "I can't put you in danger any-more, and Astir can't investigate the people that are closest to me."

"We have to go back," she whispered, pressing her cheek against his shoulder and wrapping her arms around him.

Astir must have had a plane standing by on another island, because less than an hour later, her entire security team and a team of military personnel burst into the resort's cabana, taking charge of the attackers who were still tied up, but all of them were conscious now and mut-tering threats. Calista and Goran had showered and dressed in more formal clothes, then stepped into the waiting SUVs, were driven to the airport and boarded the plane. Unfortunately, Goran kissed her cheek and said, "I need to find out who put you in danger." Then he disap-peared into the plane's conference room. Calista got on the phone with Astir, updating him, but her big, overly protective brother didn't give her any information. Of course he wouldn't, she thought with resent-ment as she paced the confines of the main cabin on the plane, fidgeting in frustration and wondering if she'd ever get any additional informa-tion. Or was she going to be relegated to being a pretty after-thought once more?

The plane landed and Calista peered out of the plane's windows, her stomach coiling with tension when she spotted the massive crowd of journalists and press gathered, eagerly awaiting their arrival.

"Great!" she muttered under her breath. Goran stepped out of the con-ference room, looking dapper and completely refreshed in an immacu-late suit. She'd pulled on a pink suit and vowed that she'd never wear pink again. Every time she wore it, she felt dismissed. She'd wear red from now on, she told herself, pulling on her public persona.

"You look lovely," Goran said, taking her hand and tucking it onto his arm. "Are you ready for this?"

Calista was never ready to face crowds. One would think she'd get used to this by now. But the terror she always felt when having to "perform" in front of a large crowd enveloped her. She lifted her chin, shifted her gaze so that they were focused just over the crowd's heads, a trick she'd learned as a child to protect herself from looking at any specific person, and nodded succinctly. "Ready," she told him.

Her fingers felt cold. Her feet hesitated slightly, but she forced them to move forward.

Goran looked down at Calista, not sure what the hell was going on. Gone was the sweet, warm, smiling woman he'd gotten to know over the past several days. The woman who had melted in his arms, kissed him everywhere, made him lose control and laughed. Where the hell was the woman who had learned to make sugar cookies? And then fought with him over the last warm cookie?

Gone, he thought. Had he only imagined that woman? He remembered her comments about being in public, about the constant criticism she faced. Yes, he'd heard her words, but he'd never realized how she changed as soon as she stepped into the public's view.

The change in her demeanor only made him more resolved to protect her.

He led her over to the stairs of the plane, determined to figure out who had kidnapped them. He vowed to put the perpetrators into prison for the rest of their miserable lives, and then figure out how to once again break through the cold, emotionless demeanor of Calista.

The cold, ice princess was back, and he didn't like it! Not one damn bit!

He looked over at his guards. The lead guard nodded and Goran acknowledged the silent signal, letting him know that the trap was in place. He and his guards, along with several of Astir's intelligence agents, had worked out a plan. They would lure the culprits out of hiding, one way or another.

Now he just had to put the plan into motion.

Ned muttered a string of expletives as he watched the television screen. The same clip had played over and over again on the news. Sheik Goran el Istra and Princess Calista del Taran had reappeared looking happy and healthy, without a care in the world. The news was talking about how the couple had escaped the public for a few days to get to know one another. There had been no mention of a kidnapping or assassination plot.

Was this good or bad news? Ned was pretty sure that he was screwed. It was only a matter of time before his participation in the plot to kidnap the leader of Skyla was discovered. Since Ned wasn't simply a participant, he was the mastermind, the punishment would be even more severe.

"Are you gonna make a run for it?"

Ned spun around, startled by the presence of Petro. Again. How the hell did the man move so silently? It was like the man was a freaking ghost!

"Why the hell would I get out of here?" Ned demanded, even though that had been his plan. He wasn't going to announce that to anyone though. Ned was very aware of what had happened to Jeffrey What's-His-Name, the guy who had failed before in Skyla! No way was Ned setting himself up for that kind of retribution for failure!

Petro shrugged. "Whatever." Ned watched the man, wanting to punch his smug face. But Ned wasn't suicidal. Punching a man like Petro was like asking to be stabbed in his sleep. Petro wouldn't put a knife to one's heart though. Nope, a man like Petro Zinhaden would stab a man in the stomach and leave him to die a long, slow, painful death. Even if a person survived one of Petro's stabbings, their body would be so damaged, life wouldn't be worth living.

"Your funeral," Petro admonished, then turned and walked out.

"Hey!" Ned called out. "Why did you come to see me?"

Petro stopped at the flap to the "door". He turned, his hands still in his pockets as he said, "I can't remember."

Ned knew that answer was bullshit! Whatever it was, Ned suspected that it had been important.

Unfortunately, Ned didn't have time to figure out what the other man was hiding. None of the men Ned had hired to kidnap Sheik el Istara were answering his calls. That alone was terrifying news. But the team of mercenaries that Ned had more recently hired to infiltrate one of the resorts they suspected the sheik was hiding out in had gone silent as well.

He glanced at the news video on his laptop, muttering several more curses. Now the bastard was walking down the stairs at the airport, looking better than ever?

Yeah, Ned's life was done.

Unless he was very smart and very fast, he thought. Rubbing a hand over the rough stubble on his jawline, Ned considered his options. He had a backup plan. He'd learned from Jeffrey's mistakes!

Chapter 11

Goran was ready to climb the walls! He needed to talk to Calista, but he couldn't put her in danger. Plus, she hadn't called him. Not a word from her in five full days! What the hell?

He remembered walking her down the stairs of the plane, feeling her ice-cold fingers on his arm. He'd tried to warm her fingers, but she'd simply pulled her hand away. They'd stood on the stage that had been set up at the airport, the podium right in front of them and she'd stepped away from him, allowing him to take the questions from the press. She'd stood two feet to the side, staring out at...he had no idea what she'd been looking at. She'd been completely blank.

Goran wanted the other Calista back! He walked into the security office, impatient now. "Any news?" he demanded.

"Nothing, Your Highness," his lead guard stated, pressing his lips together in frustration. "We've tracked everyone's movements for the past four weeks. Nothing stands out."

Goran turned, his eyes piercing Ismar, his head of security. "What does your gut tell you?" he demanded of the man. "Has anyone tried to get into the palace? Have you received any calls from the press or another country or anything that might stand out?"

"Nothing from our end, Your Highness," Ismar replied, sighing with his own frustration. "However, most of the requests for interviews and diplomatic meetings goes through your assistant."

Goran turned and looked at his assistant, Samir. "What about you? Any odd requests lately?"

Samir shook his head, his Adam's apple bobbing nervously and he shifted on his feet. "Nothing out of the ordinary, Your Highness."

Goran ran a hand through his hair, unconcerned with the muss he'd made. "Any news from Astir?" he demanded?

Again, Samir shook his head. "Not a word."

Goran couldn't believe that not even Astir had called. The man had vowed to continue his search for anything that might be out of place and Goran had appreciated his friend's offer of assistance. Astir was outside of the play of issues here in Skyla and might be more effective in ferreting out some clue. But obviously, Astir hadn't any additional news either.

Goran was ready to punch a wall and he might have, if most of the walls inside the palace weren't a foot thick and made of solid stone. The palace had been constructed centuries ago, when thick walls were the only way to protect the inhabitants from invaders.

He looked around, trying to think of something that might give him a clue. But he only found walls. Walls keeping him inside the palace. Walls.

Walls....keeping him inside.

Turning, he walked out of the security office, ignoring the startled glances of his head of security. Samir hurried, trying to keep up. "Have you thought of something?" the shorter man asked.

Goran shook his head. "No. Nothing." He ignored the other man, walking faster. His longer legs meant that Samir had to run to keep up with him, but Goran didn't slow down the way he normally would. In fact, he moved faster, needing to outpace the shorter man.

Once he was inside his private apartment, he walked over to the security wall. He pressed several buttons and a secret panel slid silently open.

A keypad opened up and Goran typed in his passcode, relieved that he remembered it. This panel had been installed so long ago, and he'd never had a reason to use it.

After the system verified his passcode, a drawer slid open. A keypad and several other tools flipped open, ready for his personal use. Including...a cell phone. He picked it up and dialed a number. Moments later, he was connected to Astir's personal line. The man answered immediately.

"Who is this?" Astir demanded.

Goran wanted to laugh, delighted with the other man's gruff voice. "It's Goran."

There was a moment's pause before Astir practically growled into the cell phone. "It's about damn time!"

Goran closed his eyes, feeling the betrayal deep down inside of his chest. "How many times have you tried to reach me recently?"

Astir sighed. "About twenty times. I was about to start using the back channels but I wasn't sure if those would work either. What the hell is going on over there?"

Goran mentally groaned but pushed the frustration out of his mind. "I just left my security team's office. They said that they'd run new background checks on everyone in the palace, going deeper than normal. But Samir, my personal assistant, was the man who oversaw that investigation. I heard him recently talking about the list of people my security team should investigate and I didn't think anything of it. But now..."

"Did your team run a background check on your assistant?"

"They wouldn't have," Goran confirmed exactly what they were both thinking.

There was another long silence as both men absorbed that information. Goran went on. "And if Samir had taken his name off of the list, then most likely, several of my security guards knew about it. None of them did anything about it. They didn't investigate him either."

"Meanwhile, there's been a lot of movement in the southern border, even going into Citran. I've contacted Zantar and he's investigating from his side of the border. That mining company that we've been looking at, they've shifted their operations into high gear, trying to hide the large pieces of equipment. But the large trucks needed to haul the materials away are more difficult to hide. They are too visible on the roads. My people have pictures, but I wasn't willing to send them to you until I'd spoken to you directly. At first, I thought that you were aware of the mining operation, but then Calista saw the pictures and explained that you hadn't approved any new mining permits after what happened here in Silar, I knew something was off. But I said that the mining company trucks were too big for your intelligence people to have ignored. They would have briefed you. Plus, there are several tents set up near the mining operations. Everything looks legit, and yet, I suspect that something isn't right."

Goran growled, fury eating at his gut like acid. Samir! His personal assistant was in on this mess! "I didn't authorize *any* of this. Even worse, I've been kept out of the loop through...hell, through digital walls set up to protect me."

There was a long pause as his friend absorbed that information. His next words were, "What the hell are you saying?"

Goran sighed, pacing back and forth as the enormity of this situation hit him. "It means that someone within my government, within the very walls of the palace, has been keeping me inside these damn walls, and keeping important information away from me."

Goran could feel the other man's fury even through the phone lines. "Okay, what do you need me to do?"

Looking around, his mind started working. "Get me the pictures you mentioned. Get them to the Silaran embassy here in Skyla. Can you get them there in the next five minutes?"

"Yes."

Goran appreciated the speed with which Astir was willing to move. "I'll get over to your embassy to pick them up. I won't have any of my guards do it since I don't know who to trust."

Astir sighed. "You'll have everything I've discovered."

"This was a conspiracy," Goran growled. "And I'm going to get to the bottom of this!"

"I will provide any help you need," Astir offered, implicitly agreeing with Goran's assessment of the situation.

Goran hesitated with his next comment, but he couldn't leave it alone. "Is Calista okay?" he asked.

The silence following that question tore at Goran's gut. "No," his friend replied. "I don't know what the hell is wrong with her, but ever since coming back from whatever hell you two went through, she hasn't really talked to me. She's not eating, she has dark circles under her eyes and..." he sighed again. "Fix this mess with your government and this damn mining company so that you can fix whatever happened between you and Calista!" A moment later, Astir ended the call.

Goran closed his eyes, his whole body prepared for battle. He needed Calista. Not just for sex, though yes, he needed to make love to her. He needed to find that passionate woman who had exploded in his arms. He needed to know that what they'd shared over those few days hadn't been a lie.

But he had to fix one mess before he could fix another. And he wouldn't go to Calista until she would be safe. He'd put her in danger once. He wouldn't do it again.

Texting Astir, he said, "*Tell her I'm fixing this! And then I'm coming to get her!*"

He stored the phone back in the secret drawer, then pressed the buttons that hid the whole panel. When everything was back to normal, he walked out of his private suite. Samir was right there, waiting for him nervously just outside of the doors to his private apartment. That only increased Goran's distrust.

"Sire, your next meeting has already convened."

Goran ignored him, heading in a different direction. But when Samir followed, Goran knew that he'd need to get rid of the man before the shorter man could cause problems.

"I need you to get a list of teachers for fourth grade students," he said, making up some ridiculous task to keep him busy elsewhere. "I need

105

the names not just of the teachers, but their education levels, where they went to school and how many of them have lived within the capital city prior to their assignments in the smaller villages." He paused and looked down at his assistant. "Can you get that to me by the end of the day?"

Samir nodded rapidly, his fingers still writing down instructions. "Absolutely, Your Highness."

Samir turned, hurrying back to his office to fulfill Goran's request. Goran then turned to his guards. He gestured for them to move closer. "I also need lists of the cleaning personnel. Specifically, the staff that clean the kitchens after hours. Can one of you do that for me?" he asked. "I'll need the same information on that cleaning staff that Samir is getting about the fourth grade teachers."

The four guards looked at each other, not sure they understood. Goran allowed his impatience to show. "Can one of you get that information? I need it immediately!"

One of the guards lifted his hand. "I'll get that information, Your Highness," he said, then immediately stepped backwards, turned, and almost ran down the hallway towards the security office.

Goran looked at the other three men. "Okay, this is the most important issue," he said, waving them all in closer. Three heads leaned in, ready for whatever he was about to say. "There's a new stable hand. I saw him in the hallway right before I left on that last trip. He was about six feet tall, which is why he caught my attention." He looked at his guards carefully, ensuring that they were all watching him closely. "Stocky fellow. There seemed to be a bulge under one of his jackets. Have any of you heard of a new stable hand?"

When all three of them shook their heads. "No, sire. We've not done any new background checks on stable hands. Not for the past year, that I know of. And none of the stable hands would be allowed access inside the palace."

Goran nodded. "That's what I thought too." He sighed, hoping that he was playing his role correctly. "Can one of you get through the palace to the stables undetected to find this person?"

The men looked at each other, concern on their features. "Your Highness, we can't leave you unguarded."

Goran shook his head, looking stern and trying to convey a sense of urgency and camraderie. "I can't let anyone in the guard office know about this." He turned to the lead guard on duty for the moment, "You heard your boss. He's already run background checks on everyone. Was this man included? And why was he allowed near the palace? Why was he hired right before I was kidnapped with Princess Calista?"

The man straightened, all of them hearing the inconsistencies. "I'll go," one of them announced. He looked at the other two. "Will you be able to protect him with just the two of you?"

"Yes!" they both replied with resounding confidence.

The man nodded, then looked at Goran. "We'll meet back here and figure out why this man wasn't fully vetted prior to his employment."

Goran put a hand on the guard's shoulder. "Thank you!" he said with sincerity. His theory was that any guard willing to go off and investigate behind the other head guard's back wasn't part of the conspiracy. However, he needed all of his guards occupied so that he could slip away to get whatever information Astir had for him. So he'd made up stories to get his guards away from him.

He could be completely off his mark on the assumption that some of his guards were part of the conspiracy. Once he had more information, he'd figure out who was part of the conspiracy and who was innocent. At the moment, everyone was guilty in his mind.

"Okay, let's go. There's more to investigate," he said to the two remaining guards. Both of them flanked him, both tall and proud and he was inclined to believe that they were both innocent. However, he wanted Calista by his side more than anything. And right now, he couldn't trust anyone. He walked all the way to his parking garage where about a hundred different vehicles were stored. There were limousines and SUVs, all of them armored. But in addition to those, which he used for official events, there were also his personal sports cars, luxury sedans, and various other types of vehicles that were used by himself and the security guards for a range of reasons.

"We're not going out," he said to the guards. "I just want to look at some of the vehicles. I think..." he sighed, rubbing the back of his head. "We'll just see what's there."

Both guards were wary, but vigilant. A good sign, he thought. He pressed the button that would take the three of them down to the parking garage.

As soon as he stepped out of the elevator, two more guards were standing at attention, ready and willing to protect.

He gestured each of them over to him. "I need everyone quiet. This can't get up to the guard room above." He waited until they were all listening intently, the two new guards resting their hands on their weapons as if ready for anything. Another good sign, he thought.

"I want each of you to look for tampering with the vehicles. Especially the vehicles that I would normally travel in. You're looking for cut wires, GPS tracking devices that shouldn't be there, tears in the material that may or may not have been sewn up." He looked at each of them carefully. "This has to be done quietly and quickly. Got it?"

They all straightened and nodded, everyone ready to do their best. He gestured to the locked key case that was stationed on the wall. The keys to every vehicle were stored in that case, which was why it was so closely guarded. "Take several keys each and let's get to it." Since Goran owned about a hundred vehicles, it would take the guards several hours to inspect each of the vehicles. Goran waited until each of the guards had taken keys to the main vehicles, then he stepped into the room and grabbed several additional keys, pretending to be helping with the inspection. Counting on them not noticing, he also grabbed the keys to one of the motorcycles that he used up in the mountains. It was a bit dirty and worn, but it would serve his purposes. While the others were busy searching through the vehicles, getting down underneath the cars, opening doors and looking under seats and in the bumpers, wheel wells, and any other place someone might place an illegal device, Goran walked over to his dirt bike, silently pushing it towards the exit. Thankfully, the exit was far enough away from the main parking garage that, when he entered the code to open the garage door, the others couldn't hear him. Moments later, he was speeding down the driveway of the palace and out through the gates. Because he was heading out of the palace, no one stopped him. Especially with his helmet covering his head.

He drove through the busy streets of the capital city, feeling a fresh surge of freedom. He hadn't ever been out through the city without his guards. It was a liberating experience but if this weren't a dire situation, he'd never risk it. But right now, his government was under threat and he had to take extreme measures.

Fifteen minutes later, Goran stuffed the envelope of satellite pictures under his shirt, then tucked his shirt back into his slacks. "Thank you!" he said to the ambassador. "I'll let Astir know that I received the information."

"Godspeed," the ambassador said, then lifted his hand to the guard, silently ordering him to open the embassy gates once again. The entire transaction had taken less than five minutes and it was only a five or ten minute drive back to the palace, depending on traffic. But Goran took an alternative route back, thinking that the guards were now alerted to his absence and would be looking for him. He wanted to be back at the palace gates before they discovered him.

He wound through the cars that were parked on the road. His driving methods weren't exactly legal, and he knew that he was presenting a very bad role model to other motorcycle drivers, but in this instance, it was more important to get back to the palace. Back to the walls, he thought. Walls that had been used to keep him inside and ignorant. But no more! And never again!

Chapter 12

"Alpha team in place."

Goran watched, his mind going through every detail of this operation, searching for errors, gaps, or vulnerabilities.

"Charlie team in place."

"Delta team in place."

There wasn't a "beta" team. Goran always chuckled when his teams refused to assign a beta team to any operation. They claimed that betas were the underdogs, and no one wanted to be on that team. Hence, they all just skipped that letter of the alphabet and moved to the others.

Samir moved in beside him and Goran looked over at Shahir, the head of the intelligence department for Skyla. The man nodded and Goran gave the "go" hand signal that had been established for this operation.

Two security guards silently slipped out of the security office.

"How is your wife?" Goran asked of Samir, both of them watching the screen as the teams moved into place.

Samir, the man who had been Goran's personal assistant for the past five months, looked up from the tablet. "She is well, Your Highness. Thank you for asking."

"She's due to give birth next week, correct?"

Samir's eyes widened. After only the briefest hesitation, the man nodded. "Yes, Your Highness. She is thirty-nine weeks pregnant."

Goran nodded, then watched the green forms move across the dark screen in front of him in infrared. His men were moving in on the mining operation. Unlike the debacle in Silar, where the mining people had scattered after the tragedy that had taken one life and destroyed almost every building in the entire village, Goran wasn't going to allow the perpetrators of this illegal mining operation to get away. These people had kidnapped him and put Calista in danger. They'd hurt her, drugged her, hit her, tied her up and, as a last resort, someone had tried to kill Calista. Goran would have issued a severe punishment for anyone who had tried to kidnap him, but since they'd involved Calista, he wasn't just angry. He was out for revenge!

"It must be frightening, anticipating a new baby."

Samir once again lifted his head. "Not really. She is healthy and the sonograms have shown that the baby is developing well."

The offered excuse for Samir's betrayal was the last possible reason Goran could think of that would mitigate the man's actions. The man had conspired with the enemy. Not just during the kidnapping, but the cover up after the fact. Shahir had also found evidence that Samir had conspired to hide information from Goran in the weeks before the kidnapping attempt as well as impeded the investigation after his return.

The green silhouettes on the screen moved closer, the outline of the tents now visible on the screen.

While Samir frantically tapped out something on his tablet, Goran watched as one member of the Charlie team bent low and pushed something underneath the bottom of the tent. Not even a whisper of sound would warn the occupants of the tent about what was happening.

The other two teams were performing identical actions on the other two tents. Everyone waited five minutes, then the teams moved in, gas masks in place and weapons ready. But as they moved through the interior of the tents, no one stirred. Everyone inside the tent was sound asleep and wouldn't wake up until the sleeping gas wore off in about ten hours. By the time they woke up, every one of them would be in a jail cell.

Just in time to be interrogated. By that point, Goran anticipated several of them to turn on their bosses and coworkers in exchange for a lighter sentence.

When it was all over, Samir sighed and flipped his tablet closed. "I'd better go and check on-"

"Just a moment," Goran interrupted his assistant. He nodded to the intelligence head and the man pressed a few buttons on a keyboard. Moments later, a series of text messages showed on the screen.

"Care to explain these messages?" Isamir asked.

Samir looked up at the large screen, his eyes bugging wide as he read the messages he'd been typing while watching the raid happen. *"Get out! Skylar forces are moving in!" "You've been caught! Get out!" "There are three teams moving closer! Why aren't you responding?!" "Get out! Get out!" "This silence isn't going to save you! Just respond so I know that you've received this message!" "You are being gassed! Get out of the tents!"*

Goran lifted his eyebrows, waiting.

Samir's mouth fell open as horror pushed through his brain. "I can explain!" he whispered, terror making his voice crack.

"I'd like to hear those explanations," Goran replied smoothly. "But not at this time." He turned, nodding to the guards. "These men are going to take you to a cell. Your home has been searched. Your office as well. Your bank accounts have been frozen. So that huge deposit that arrived earlier this morning from a Caribbean bank isn't going to help you. Not anymore."

Samir swallowed, trying to back up. His eyes looked to the right, then the left, desperate for an escape route.

"There is no escape, Samir. Every exit to the palace has been shut down."

The stupid man still tried to rush the guards. Seconds after that attempt, the two guards had Samir flat on his stomach with his hands pulled behind his back and handcuffs pinching the skin on his wrists.

Samir tried to yell, to explain, but Goran didn't want to hear the traitor's excuses. Not anymore. He'd let his security team deal with Samir. Right now, all he wanted to do was to find Calista and explain why he hadn't been able to contact her. It was all because this bastard had been intercepting and re-routing phone calls in order to keep Goran from getting any additional information!

Chapter 13

He hadn't called. Calista stared out the window of the dining room, her fingers cold as she contemplated the next few hours in the company of Rachel and Astir. For the past several weeks, she'd endured their pitying glances, knew that Rachel and Astir sometimes held hands under the table and she had walked in on the two of them too many times in each other's arms. They were in a cocoon of nauseating happiness and...!

That wasn't fair. Rationally, Calista was very happy for Astir. He deserved to have found happiness with Rachel. It wasn't that she disliked Rachel. Calista just hated that she wasn't happy.

And now...now...now she knew that she was pregnant. It wasn't really a mystery as to how that had happened. She simply hadn't...calculated the dates correctly. It must have happened that first time. It had been so magical, so passionate. Neither of them had even thought about contraception until afterwards.

But now she was two weeks late.

"*'Ahlan.*"

Calista turned to find Ayla standing a few feet away from her. "*'Ahlan,*" she replied, trying to force a smile. Unfortunately, the pain was too deep for even a pretend smile.

"What's wrong?" Ayla asked softly, coming to stand closer. "Something happened during your kidnapping, didn't it?"

Calista tilted her head. "You mean, besides falling in love with the man I was supposed to marry, only to find myself ignored now that we're safe?"

Ayla's beautiful eyes widened and she stepped closer, taking Calista's free hand. "Oh, Calista!"

Calista sighed, leaning her head against Ayla's. "Thank you for giving me some space over the past couple of weeks since I came back." She blinked back tears. "I know that you were scared for me, and then confused when I came back and didn't..."

"Hush!" Ayla whispered. "You don't have to apologize to me. I could see the confusion in your eyes." They stood like that for a while until Calista sniffed.

"I need to be strong," she told Ayla. "But I'll be okay."

"What's wrong?" a deep, masculine voice demanded, interrupting their conversation.

Calista and Ayla jerked apart, turning to look at their older brother.

"Wrong?" she asked, trying to pull herself together. She pasted a smile on her features and pulled her shoulders back. "Nothing is wrong."

Ayla hugged Calista. "I'll give you two some privacy," and then she was gone, leaving Calista to face her brother alone.

Astir glared at her, barely waiting for Ayla to close the door on her departure before he shook his head. "You're lying. And I don't know if you're doing it to protect me or if you're genuinely trying to convince yourself." He moved closer. "Either way, I can see that you're miserable. Why don't you just tell me what's on your mind?"

Calista set the untouched glass of wine on the table. She couldn't drink wine any longer. Not with her pregnancy. Besides, the wine didn't taste right. That was probably another sign of her pregnancy, but she'd been too oblivious lately to realize that nothing tasted right. Nothing felt right either. Her clothes were too tight. Her body felt...off in so many ways.

"I'm fine," she told her older brother. Calista stood up and looked around. "Where's Rachel?"

Astir's hands fisted on his hips as he glared down at her. "You're not fine. I asked Rachel to give me some time alone with you so I could find out what is going on." He moved closer, his eyes shifting from furious to concerned. "Is it Goran? Did he do something to hurt you?"

Pain lashed her with his words and Calista briefly closed her eyes. When she opened them again, Astir was still staring at her. "I'm fine," she told him, then laid her hand on his arm, trying to reassure him even though she didn't feel very reassuring. "I think I'm going to pass on dinner tonight. I'm tired."

"Calista, what the hell happened to you last month?"

She stopped, her shoulders tightening with dread. "I've told you, Astir. Nothing happened. We were kidnapped. But the guards didn't hurt me in any way. Other than being drugged that first night, we escaped and were pretty much alone and safe for the rest of the time until they found us at the resort." She smiled at the memory. "You should know that since it was your guards who picked them up."

"I know that. But I still want to know if something else happened. You were with Goran for several days. Alone. What happened?"

"We cooked. We did a lot of swimming. We went for a hike through the jungle." She smiled slightly, ignoring the shaft of pain. "We saw a beautiful waterfall. We went to the local market every day to buy food and the resort delivered the other meals to us." She shrugged. "Basically, we kept to ourselves and...talked." That last word was spoken with a slight quiver. It was the truth. She and Goran had talked. A lot! And she'd fallen in love with the man.

Then...they'd come back to reality. After walking off the plane on his arm, she hadn't seen or spoken to Goran.

Her brother looked at her carefully. "There was a time, before you and he were taken, that I thought you were going to break off your engagement with him. I was wrong, wasn't I?"

Calista shook her head. "No. Before that incident, I..." she hesitated. Had she hated Goran? No. She'd disliked him. "Before that week in Costa Rica, we were strangers. We didn't really know each other then. And I haven't heard from him since."

"I think there's more to his silence, Calista," Astir replied. "There's something going on and I suspect that...well, I'm not sure. And I think it would be better coming from Goran." He put a hand on her shoulder, his dark eyes looking down into hers. "Don't give up on him. He's coming back to you."

A flood of memories of their week together swept through her mind. Sadness filled her, pain in her heart at Goran's silence now. "I have to go," Calista told her brother, turning quickly away from his too-knowing eyes.

Everything she'd said to her brother was true. Before that week, she'd honestly disliked Goran. They'd shared one, amazing kiss. But every other interaction between them had been tedious. It had convinced her that they weren't compatible.

Then some bastard in Goran's government had helped a mining company executive that had decided that Goran needed to be taken out of the picture for a short period of time. Just long enough for the mining contracts to be signed and mining operations initiated. But more importantly, the kidnapping had thrown the Skyla government into chaos. Nothing was getting done. No one was looking at the illegal trucks coming and going along the border roads, so the mining operation could continue without any oversight.

Thankfully, the mining operators had been stopped and the caves where the trucks were going into and out of were barred from further operations. The government was back under control and very few people knew what had actually happened.

He was a good man, she thought, reaching for the door handle. But moments before her fingers would have touched it, the door opened, surprising her enough that she had to step backwards.

"Calista!" Goran burst out, stepping into the room.

Calista froze, not sure if her eyes were tricking her. The tall, gorgeous man standing in front of her was...it couldn't be him! "Goran? What...?" She stopped when he pulled her into his arms. Closing her eyes, she savored this moment, but confusion won out over her elation at seeing him again. Pulling back, she stared up at him, but wouldn't release him. "What are you doing here?"

"I'm here because you're a stubborn, annoying woman who wouldn't call me. So I took the situation into my own hands." She stepped out of his arms, then backed up a step when she realized that his emotions had shifted from elation at seeing her to...anger? Why would he be angry? What right did he have to be angry with her? Shouldn't she be angry with him? Shouldn't she be telling him off? Or...maybe she should tell him about the baby they'd created together.

Unfortunately, none of those words made it from her mind to her lips. She took another step back, stunned by all of the emotions rippling through her at the moment. But Goran hadn't ever let her get away with retreat. He'd challenged her at every opportunity. Instead of halting and allowing her the time to get a grip on what was going on, he stepped forward, invading her space.

"What are you doing?" she demanded, but her voice didn't sound as firm and indignant as she'd hoped. In fact, she sounded...hopeful! Oh, that simply wasn't going to work!

"I'm going to..." he stopped, looking over her shoulder. Suddenly, Calista was painfully aware of Astir still in the room.

"I was wondering if anyone was going to notice that I was still here," he muttered dryly, obviously uncomfortable. "But since both of you are blocking the only exit, I'm afraid that I can't really...uh...leave both of you alone to work out whatever the hell is wrong with both of you." He rubbed the back of his neck. "Although, it goes against my better judgement to leave my baby sister alone with a man who obviously has salacious intentions towards her."

Goran glared at Astir and, since Calista was staring at her brother as well, her mind working hard to try and figure out what was going on, she didn't see Goran step closer. And she didn't see his arm whip out to wrap around her waist until it was too late and it pulled her against Goran's side. Her hand snapped up, pressing against his chest to balance herself, but she shouldn't have bothered. Goran's arm held her firmly against his side as he continued to glare at Astir.

"Give us a few minutes to sort this out. I promise that…"

Astir lifted his hand. "I don't want to know your plans," he warned. "If you tell me what you're going to do, I'll have to stop you." He sighed, shaking his head. "Just promise me that your intentions are honorable and I'll get the hell out of here and let you deal with it."

Goran's body stiffened for a brief moment, but then he relaxed and nodded. "My intentions are honorable. And the faster you get out, the faster I can convince her to marry me."

Astir chuckled. "I thought that you already did that. You guys have been engaged for a while now, if you'll both remember." But Astir stepped around the couple, moving through the doors and pulling them closed behind him.

Goran turned, looking down at Calista. "We were engaged," he confirmed. "But that was a legal document. We both agreed to the engagement. However," his hands settled on her hips and he looked at her carefully. "Calista, I want you to marry me because you love me. Because you can't imagine life without me."

"You do?"

"Yes," he replied softly, his voice gruff as he leaned closer. "After being with you in Costa Rica, I got to know you. The real person behind all of the tense public appearances. I want that woman. I love that woman."

She sighed, shaking her head. "The problem is, I'm both. I endure painful, sometimes debilitating stage fright, Goran. I deal with it because I have to. I put on the persona in front of strangers and the cameras because this is the life I've been born into. But…that's me, just as much as the woman who learned to bake cookies and laugh and talk with you. It's all the same person." She licked her lips, staring up at him. "I'm both. I can't separate the two people."

He kissed her briefly. "Can I have the relaxed woman when we're alone?" he suggested.

She licked her lips, her eyes dropping to his mouth. "Yes," she whispered. "But I can't guarantee that the woman will disappear immediately after every public appearance. It takes time for one persona to transform into the other," she explained. "Depending on the size of the crowds, my stomach sometimes becomes quite upset and it takes me a while to get over the sensation." She smoothed her hands up to rest against his shoulders. "I can't guarantee which version of me you'll see at any moment."

"I'll take them both," he told her, pulling her closer. "And you don't have to go out in public, Calista. That's not necessary. Especially if it makes you ill."

She laughed, shaking her head. "You can't eliminate all of my public appearances."

"I can," he declared with absolute finality.

She smiled now, finding his protection endearing. "Goran, we got out of the car after Costa Rica and there was a massive crowd there to greet us. I froze. I froze them out and I froze you out. I can't help it. When I'm around strangers, I just...freeze. I look cold and evil. And the last time, I froze you out as well."

He shrugged. "Now that I know it's just your fears kicking in, I can handle it. Before, I thought it was me that you were trying to freeze out. That's different." He kissed her, his hands sliding down over her hips. "I'm pretty sure that I'll do something that will make you crazy too."

Her relief was huge. "You really want me for myself?" she asked, those old insecurities still hidden but just as vicious.

"Every part of you, love," he promised. "I want the whole package."

Her smile brightened. "You do?"

He chuckled. "As long as you're willing to accept me as well. All the good and the burned parts."

She laughed, lifting up onto her toes as she hugged him. "It's a deal!" she replied, excited and thrilled and a whole host of other emotions. When she pulled back, he started to kiss her, but she placed a hand on his mouth.

"Wait!" she erupted.

"Wait?" He looked confused and she noticed the anger forming in his eyes. "For what?" He bristled slightly. "Calista, you know that I'm taking you back to Skyla tonight, right? We'll be married by the weekend."

She gasped, shaking her head. "No! I can't do that!"

"Why the hell not?" he grumbled, releasing her but his hands fisted on his hips. She recognized his "battle mode" now and smiled, reassured despite his increasing frustration.

"Because I want my sister at my wedding," she told him, unwilling to budge on that issue. "And Astir along with Rachel. I want my family there with me."

Goran ran a hand over his face, sighing with increasing ire. "Calista, I need you. I need you by my side. I need to know that you're safe and under my protection. I need you in my country, in my home so that I can protect you." He moved closer, pulling her against him again. "I need you in my bed."

Her heart warmed with those words and she smiled. "I want all of that too. But...I really need my family at my wedding." She snuggled against him. "I'm fine being with you. In fact, I think we have a lot to talk about and it would be best if we weren't here during those conversations."

He looked down at her, but his arms tightened around her. "You'll come back with me tonight?" he grumbled.

"Yes."

"And you'll be in my bed? You'll act as my fiancée until we can officially be married?"

She smiled at his uncompromising tone. "Yes."

"Good."

"We'll do it all together." She hesitated, her face resting against his chest. She could hear his heart beating and smiled. "We'll even go see the doctor together."

His heart sped up and every muscle in his body froze. Then he pulled away, his hands tightening on her upper arms as he bent to look into her eyes. "What's wrong? Are you sick?"

Calista laughed, shaking her head. "No. I'm not sick. But remember that first night at the resort?" she asked, then shrugged. "Well, our first morning. When I did that...thing to you and it sort of made both of us lose control?"

"Yes. What about...?" he stopped. A moment later, he swallowed hard, still staring at her.

"Right," she said, licking her lips. "Well, you have to understand that I was a bit out of sorts. So the counting the days thing...well, I was pretty off." She saw his face transform and lifted a hand to his chest. "In my defense, we'd gone through a pretty rough time!" she blurted out. "And...and I didn't realize that my calculations were off by more than a week. I was flustered and confused and if I'd had a calendar with me, I might have been more accurate. But..."

"You're pregnant?" he whispered harshly, his hands tightening on her upper arms almost painfully.

"Yes."

"And you didn't call me immediately?"

She shrugged. "Well, at first, I was so sad that you didn't come and talk to me. We'd been through so much during that time together. And I thought...!"

"I thought you were done with me!" he growled, releasing her arms and starting to pace. "First of all, my assistant was blocking my calls. I wasn't getting any information at all. But also, you froze up on me and I didn't hear from you."

"I only froze up on you because of the crowds," she inserted. "I explained all of that to you."

"Yes, but at the time, I didn't know that." More pacing and he ran a hand through his hair. "I thought you were just...freezing me out. Just like before."

"No. I wasn't. And then, I was hurt that you didn't know that about me. But then I realized that you couldn't know how much I suffer from stage fright. I'd mentioned it, but I don't know if I conveyed just how serious my fears become. Every time we'd been together, it had been either right before or right after a public appearance."

He stared at her, his mind seeming to go back in time. Then relief surged through him. His eyes cleared and he rushed towards her again. "You're pregnant?"

"Yes," she replied, nodding as if he needed the extra confirmation.

"Are you okay?" he asked. He looked down over her figure. "You've lost weight. You need to eat more."

Calista laughed. "I was lonely, so yeah, I haven't been eating well." She lifted up onto her toes and kissed him gently. "But now that you're here, I feel much better. And I promise to eat better."

"Good," he grumbled, pulling her against his chest and resting his head on top of hers. "I'll take care of you."

She smiled, hugging him closer. "I'll take care of you too," she whispered back, closing her eyes as if silently vowing to make that promise come true.

"I love you!"

Calista hadn't realized that she'd been waiting to hear those words until he uttered them. The rush of emotions brought tears to her eyes as she replied, "I love you, too!"

Epilogue

"No, you can't eat Pablo's dog food," Calista said to her five year old son. Timar glared at the dog's bowl and Pablo glared back. Obviously, this was an ongoing battle between the child and his four-legged best friend.

"But why not?" Timar demanded.

Goran stepped into the dining room, lifting Timar up into the air with a growl. Instantly, Timar's disgruntlement broke into giggles as his father nibbled on his tummy. Finally, Goran rolled his son around so that they were looking at each other eye to eye. "You can't eat the dog's food because you don't have fur!"

Timar and Goran both looked down to find the dog staring happily up at the duo, his tail wagging so hard that the back end of his body wagged with it.

"But maybe if I eat Pablo's food, then I'll grow fur." His eyes widened as an idea struck him. "Maybe I can even grow a tail."

Pablo barked, unwilling to be ignored.

Goran set his son back down on the floor, then rubbed Pablo's rough fur. "That's not how it works. And if you steal all of Pablo's food, then maybe his tail will fall off. We wouldn't want that, would we?"

Timar looked appropriately horrified at that idea that he knelt on the floor, hugging his faithful companion. "I won't eat your food!" he promised with all the solemnity that only a five year old could convey.

Goran walked over to Calista, bending down to nibble on her neck with a bit less fanfare than the tummy nibbling moments ago. "And how are you?" he asked, resting his hand on her swollen belly.

"Don't ask," she grumbled, shifting on her chair.

Timar moved back onto his chair, grabbing his fork and stabbing a piece of watermelon. "Momma said you're in trouble."

Goran sat down in the empty chair, flipping his linen napkin over his lap as one of the servants poured coffee for him. "And why am I in trouble?" he asked, looking over at his wife with amusement.

"You know exactly why you're in the doghouse!" she muttered, thinking of the previous night when he'd teased and toyed with her until she was almost desperate for release.

"I wanna be in the doghouse!" Timar called out, brightening at the possibility.

Goran laughed, not saying a word as he took a sip of his coffee. "I didn't hear you complaining last night."

She rolled her eyes. "Then you weren't paying attention."

He threw back his head, laughing with delight at his beautiful wife.

"Can I live in the doghouse with Pablo?" Timar asked, his eyebrows tightening as his confusion over the conversation increased. "If Daddy can do it, then why can't I?"

Calista looked over at her husband, smiling as she lifted her eyebrows, silently telling him that he must answer their son.

Goran turned, looking at Timar. "How about if you and I try and build a doghouse-like structure that will go around your bed?"

Timar sat up straighter in his chair, absently reaching down to touch Pablo, whose tail began wagging again. "Really? Could we really do that?"

Goran shrugged. "I don't see why not. Your momma thinks I can do anything."

Timar's face broke out into a huge grin and he nodded. "I think you're a hero too!" He wiggled off of his chair and raced over to his father's seat. Goran lifted his tiny son up into his arms, settling him onto his lap. "Momma says it all the time!" he whispered.

Goran looked over at his wife, his glance telling her that he loved her. Reaching out, his fingers touched hers and Calista knew that her world was absolutely perfect at that moment.

A message from Elizabeth:
I always write the story and then title the book. When I finished the second draft of this story, I sat back, trying to figure out an appropriate title for the book. I initially came up with "The Sheik's Rescue" but hesitated. In all of my stories, I try to make the female characters strong and confident. That title implies that Goran did all of the "rescuing" in this plot and I didn't like taking the credit away from Calista, who was pivotal to every aspect of the escape scene.

However, I decided to go with it when I realized the title could mean two things at once. The sheik could be doing the rescuing, or he could be the one being rescued. *My feminist mind still jumped to images of a tall, dark, and handsome champion. But the title can be interpreted either way. It's unfortunate that our minds are taught to think of the male doing the saving of the heroine. So I offer the challenge to each of you. When you read the title, did you ever think of Calista saving Goran?*

I don't know if I'm correct about the title, but it was an interesting mental conundrum.

Regardless, I hope that you enjoyed the story – not as a feminist treatise, but merely as a happy escape from the challenges of our daily lives.

And – as usual – I'm requesting reviews. Every time I release a book to the world, I sit at my desk waiting, refreshing the book page, tense and anxious until I read your reviews. It isn't until I see the comments each of you leave that I finally relax (and sometimes take notes for future stories). Go back to your favorite retailer to the book page – and I thank you!

(As usual, if you don't want to leave feedback in a public forum, feel free to e-mail me directly at elizabeth@elizabethlennox.com. I answer all e-mails personally, although it sometimes takes me a while. Please don't be offended if I don't respond immediately. I tend to lose myself in writing stories and have a hard time pulling my head out of the book.)

Elizabeth

(Keep scrolling for a fun excerpt from next month's "The Sheik's Siren"!)

Excerpt from "The Sheik's Siren"
Release Date: June 10, 2022

2nd Note from Elizabeth: Faye and Zantar weren't part of the original series plan – so I know that the story might feel out of place initially – but I guarantee that their story "fits" into the overall plan.

The harsh sounds of multiple cars crashing and glass breaking pulled his eyes away from the report he'd been reading. Looking out the window, Sheik Zantar Al Abouss glanced around, feeling the sudden tension of his guards as they all went on high alert, trying to figure out why traffic had come to a sudden halt. His armored SUV was not part of the accident, but there were four cars ahead that were badly mangled.

"I'll see what's going on," one of the guards said, stepping out of the vehicle. The man stepped onto the sidewalk and looked around, moving several feet down the road.

Once again, Zantar looked out the window and...couldn't believe his eyes! A woman was on the beach in the most bizarre pose he'd ever seen. In fact, he wasn't even sure how she'd gotten her arms and legs into that pose! Her legs were in the air, her hands down in the sand. Her head was...he wasn't sure. Slowly, her long, sexy legs lowered to the sand and she stood up, her very delectable derriere leading the way.

The guard who had stepped out of the SUV to investigate the traffic jam came back with an irritated huff. "It's the woman!" he snarled, jerking his thumb towards the woman behind him. "She distracted the drivers up ahead. In fact, the four drivers of the crashed vehicles are standing on the side of the road, watching the woman." The guard huffed and looked over his shoulder, even tilting his head slightly as the woman in question moved into a different yoga position. "What the hell is she doing?"

Zantar threw back his head, laughing at the beautiful scenario. The woman was merely exercising, completely oblivious to the chaos around her. She had no idea that the relatively conservative country of Skyla wasn't ready for a woman in skintight clothing to be moving in that manner. His country of Citran was a bit more liberal, but the woman's figure was enticing enough that the men in his country would probably have the same reaction.

Even as he watched, the woman centered herself, put her hands in front of her chest, palms together, eyes closed and went very still. No one moved. It seemed as if no one even breathed as everyone watched...silently waiting. A brief moment later, the lovely woman sighed and nodded, her hands lowering to her lap.

Entranced, Zantar's laughter was long forgotten as the woman stood up, lifted her face to the early morning sunshine, and smiled! A second later, she threw her hands up in the air as if she were somehow trying to hug the sunshine! Or the waves? He wasn't sure. Maybe both.

A moment later, she turned and his breath caught in his throat as he stared at her lovely face. She pulled the band out of her hair and the ocean breeze pulled the strands higher, lifting the soft, brown locks into the air, swooping it all around her face. She wasn't bothered. The woman simply pulled her hair out of her eyes and bent down, picking up a long skirt. She wrapped it around her tiny waist, then rolled up her yoga mat, stuffed it into a bag and walked up the beach to the sidewalk.

Zantar was captivated. Completely enraptured by the beauty of the woman. No, not just her beauty. He'd been with many beautiful women over the years. It wasn't just her full, soft lips or the delicate line of her jaw. It wasn't her now-covered derriere or her full breasts, hidden by a loose shirt, yet still visible when she bent down to slide sandals onto her feet.

There was something more, something different and alluring about the woman. He wanted her. Zantar knew that his desires were impossible. He was only here visiting Sklya because of some mysterious issue that the Sheik of Skyla and the Sheik of Silar needed to discuss with him. The fact that both men had asked him to visit and that the meetings would include three of the most powerful leaders in their region was enough for Zantar to realize that something significant was happening.

Pulling his eyes away from the woman, Zantar tried to focus back on his reports. He didn't bother to glance at his watch. He didn't have time, and yet, a moment later, he reached for the door handle and stepped out of the vehicle. His guards instantly moved to surround him but he waved a hand, silently telling them to spread out as he moved towards the woman walking along the beach. It wasn't as if his guards could move the SUVs. The four-car pileup ensured that the people on the street weren't going anywhere. The traffic was completely snarled now. It was going to take several tow trucks and the police taking statements to get this situation cleared out before he could be on his way. He might as well put the delay to good use.

"Good morning," he called out.

Instantly, the woman stopped, her loose-limbed walk halting as she stared up at him from six feet away.

"Who are you?" the woman demanded, squinting up at him now that the sun was higher over the horizon.

"You may call me Zantar," he replied, sliding his hands into his pockets to keep them from reaching out to pull her closer. She was even more stunning close up. Her light blue eyes were surrounded by thick, dark lashes. Her skin was tanned, but he suspected that was due to the sun rather than heredity. And her lips...damn her mouth was full and sensuous, wide and curving up at the corners even as she looked at him warily.

She hesitated for a moment, her mouth opening slightly as if she were as caught up in the awareness of him as he was with her. Good, he thought, even more intrigued.

"Good morning, Zantar," she said softly. She took another step closer, then halted. "You're very tall!"

He lifted a dark eyebrow. "And you're very dangerous," he replied.

Her eyes widened. "I am?" Those lips curved into a smile. "I think I like the idea of being dangerous." She stepped closer again. "How am I dangerous? Do I look mysterious?"

He chuckled, shaking his head, but he pulled one hand out of his pocket as he pointed behind her at the crash site, two of the men still standing on the sidewalk watching her.

She looked over her shoulder, then her head swiveled back to him. "The accident?"

"Yes, *eazizi*," he replied, his voice deeper now, as he realized that she was unaware of the impact she had on men. On him!

Her head tilted slightly and it seemed as if she were concentrating. "That means..." she pressed her lips together for a moment, then shook her head. "I'm sorry. I've only started to learn your language. I'm not familiar with that word."

His lips curled slightly and he was suddenly startled to discover that she was American. They'd been speaking in English this whole time but he'd been so distracted by her mouth and those blue eyes, he hadn't even realized it. He should have assumed her country of origin based on the casual style of her hair and the loose feel of her clothing. Perhaps he would have noticed those details, but her eyes...they were quite startling. And her mouth was wide and full and...luscious.

"Where are you off to?" he asked, ignoring her question about the translation. He'd called her "my dear", and even he was surprised by the intimacy implied by that term.

Her confusion dissipated and her features brightened as she smiled up at him. "I'm going to grab a cup of coffee at that small coffee shop over there," she explained, pointing towards the corner shop with green umbrellas and metal chairs. "And then I have to hurry off to work."

He contemplated her for a moment, his eyes glancing behind her once again. There was no movement at the crash site, so he made a snap decision. "I will join you for coffee," he announced.

The woman's body seemed to jerk slightly, but her smile brightened even more. "You will? Well, I'm so glad that I invited you to join me then!" she replied with a teasing smile.

Zantar grunted slightly, not sure how he felt about her teasing. For some reason, he liked it. But he didn't want to like it. She was...cute. And sexy. And enticing. It was startling that she already felt comfortable enough to tease him. Or was that just part of her personality? For some reason, he didn't like that thought. He preferred thinking that this fascinating woman...what? Was his? He'd just met her!

However, when she started walking again, her stride long and confident and her blue eyes twinkling up at him, he felt a possessive surge rise up inside of him.

It was just coffee, he reminded himself. And yet, when she stepped closer as they walked along the sidewalk, his hand moved to the small of her back.

Faye felt his hand and looked up at him, startled by the intense heat emanating from the man. His hand scorched her skin through her shirt but...that was impossible, right?

"I'm Faye, by the way," she told him.

He looked down at her, his dark eyes sharp, seeming to take in details that she knew nothing about. "That is a very pretty name, Faye," he replied.

He pronounced her name as if it were a lullaby. Something melted inside of her and she smiled up at him. This day just kept getting better and better, she thought. "Why did you imply that I was the cause of the accident back there?" she said, gesturing absently with her hand to the area that was now behind them.

"You were doing yoga on the beach," he explained, his voice deep and gravelly.

She chuckled. "Let's just examine this for a moment," Faye said, stopping and smiling when he stopped as well. "You're saying that I'm the cause of the accident. And yet, I was minding my business over there on the beach. The subjects of the accident are the four men who weren't paying attention to where they were going."

"And yet, you were the distraction."

Again, Faye shook her head. "*They* were distracted. *I* was not distracting them. I was not an active participant in their distraction. You are saying that men are too weak to concentrate. If that's true, if men are too easily distracted, then perhaps they should not be allowed to drive."

He didn't respond to that and Faye's features brightened even more. Finally, he grunted, and Faye wasn't sure if that was acceptance of her argument or a dismissal because her comments didn't fall into place with the normal arguments that women should always cover up to avoid being a "temptation" to men.

She squinted up at him, trying to translate that sound. "Were you a bear in a past life?" she asked.

Printed in Great Britain
by Amazon

19450584R00077